THE SILENT WITNESS

A LIGHTHOUSE KEEPER'S SECRET

STEVEN JACOBS

OTHER WORKS BY THE AUTHOR

ALSO BY STEVEN JACOBS

THE SILENT WITNESS

A Lighthouse Keepers Secret

A work of Fiction
By Steven Jacobs

To my family and friends who have supported me in this endeavor of putting my stories down on paper.

Special Thanks to Gregg Beck, who provided the photo from which the cover was made.

"I'm not working on The Great American Novel. All I'm doing, I hope, is entertaining readers."
Clive Cussler

PROLOGUE

The Present

Luke stepped out of the lawyer's office onto the sidewalk, took a deep breath, and said, "I'm glad that's over with."

"Are you okay?" Lisa, his wife of nine years, asked as she wrapped her arm around him while they walked to the car.

"Yeah, I'm okay, I guess. I'm still trying to understand all of this. I can't believe it's really happening," Luke replied.

"Well, believe it because it's happening. Trust me, I was in there while we just signed our life away for the past hour," Lisa said with a giggle.

"We didn't sign our life away, silly," Luke said with a smile. "It may have felt like it, but all we really did was transfer the deed of the property from my parent's estate to us. That's all. We now officially own the lighthouse, and we're free to turn it into a bed and breakfast."

Lisa smiled and said, "I know it's hard to believe. I can't wait!"

"Neither can I," Luke said excitedly as he wrapped his arms around her petite frame and gave her a squeeze. The two were the exact opposites in stature. Luke was over six feet tall, and Lisa barely cracked five feet. Whenever she hugged him, he would always give her a little pat on the top of the head. She acted like it aggravated her, but deep down, she liked it.

Luke said, "After Congress passed the Lighthouse Preservation Act and since the General Service Administration decided to put it up for sale, we were given the first crack at it since my family has run the lighthouse since my ancestors immigrated here after the First World War."

"I am almost as excited as you are," Lisa said. I mean, think about it. It was our first trip together. We were married there, and it was just a beautiful place. I would hate to think about another family owning it."

Luke held up a large, fairly thick manila envelope and said, "Well, now, thanks to what's in here, we will never have to think about that. All we have to do now is renovate and get it ready for guests and weddings."

"Well, at least we only live thirty minutes away. That way, we can still live where we are while we do most of the renovations," Lisa said.

"I know. It's a good thing the family created a trust years ago for the lighthouse. It will pay for the renovations and then some. I'm glad, too, because I hate our current apartment."

"I know, sweetie, but we're on our way, and it won't be too long before we can say goodbye to this place and live at the lighthouse for the rest of our lives."

SIX MONTHS LATER, the lighthouse and attached two-story home renovations were in full swing. The original lighthouse keeper's home was fully modernized with new wiring, an updated kitchen, bathroom, living spaces, and even an office for working guests.

The lighthouse itself was given a new coat of paint, its broken windows replaced, and the old lantern removed. For those guests who were brave enough to make the trek to the top, a plush bench-style seat was installed almost all the way around the lantern room for guests to take in the scenery, take pictures, or just read in peace and quiet.

One day, while workers were repairing an interior wall in the main house, they accidentally found a hollow area in the wall. After opening the hollow area a little more and shining a light in the space to see why it was there, the workers were shocked to see a sizeable recessed shelf with books still on it.

After notifying Luke and Lisa about the discovery, the crew worked carefully for the next hour or more to uncover the decades-old, recessed bookshelf and carefully retrieve the books. As Luke carefully thumbed through several of the books, he was amazed to see that most were journals written by his great-grandfather Christof, the first Wolf family member to run the lighthouse.

Once all the books were removed, Luke and Lisa decided they would like to preserve the bookshelf and eventually type out what turned out to be years' worth of journal entries, which would be printed into a book adding immensely to the lighthouse's history.

Later that night, Lisa said, "I wonder why they were sealed up in the wall like they were."

"I have no idea, really. I've always heard rumors of a family journal around, but I don't think anybody ever expected something like this," Luke said, still flabbergasted as he looked at over a dozen different books, all of which were apparently written by Christof Wolf, his great-great-grandfather.

"Maybe there's something juicy in there!" Lisa said with a giggle, "Nothing like one-hundred-year-old gossip!"

"I doubt it, but right now, that's the cool thing about those old journals. There is no telling what's in there," Luke admitted.

"Isn't that the truth," Lisa said, "There's gotta be a reason they were sealed up in the wall, that's for sure."

"Yeah, well ... that's kinda what I'm afraid of," Luke replied.

"Why's that?" Lisa asked.

"What if the stories I've always heard about my ancestors are true?" Luke asked.

"What if they're not?" Lisa shot back, "You would be able to set the record straight."

"True, though I doubt it would matter anymore," Luke retorted.

As the day came to a close, Luke and Lisa gently loaded the newly found journals into the car for the half-hour drive back into the city. While Lisa drove, Luke looked for the earliest journal he could find and began studying the handwriting to see if he could decipher it.

A little more than ten minutes into the ride back home, Luke said, "My Lord! This is unbelievable! I can read everything almost perfectly. The details are so real as if I'm actually experiencing them. This is incredible. No wonder there were so many different journals."

"Read me some I wanna hear!" Lisa said excitedly.

Luke said, "Okay, but don't say I didn't warn you. The more I read this, the more I'm starting to realize it was written as if he were writing a novel. Maybe he was trying to turn his experiences into a book!"

"Well! Read it to me, damn it!" Lisa said eagerly.

"I'm getting to it. You make sure you keep your eyes on the road. Here goes nothing," Luke said as he began to read.

Lisa drove and listened to Luke as her mind wandered back in time over a hundred years ago ... to the First World War.

JUNE 1918

Just after sunrise, Wilhelm was keeping watch from their fighting position in the tree line when he began to see figures slowly emerging from the early morning fog. "Christof ... Christof, get up. I see movement out there," his friend, Wilhelm, said as he woke the sleeping Christof with his foot at the bottom of their fortified fighting position.

Yawning, Christof said, "Damn Americans, I was dreaming about Anna too!" Christof slowly eased up to the observation slit so he could have a look for himself. Christof could not believe what he saw as he peered across the field. Slowly, several ranks of Americans were coming out of the fog and advancing directly at them in skirmish lines.

Christof said incredulously, "The Americans didn't even try to scout the woods! They don't know we're here! The fools!"

Immediately up and down the line, the rest of Christof's regiment realized what was happening, took their positions, and waited for the order to open fire. The regiment waited a few tense moments for the Americans to advance within thirty meters of their lines. Suddenly, the regiment opened up, firing into the American ranks with everything they had, killing many of the approaching troops before they even realized what was happening.

Christof and Wilhelm fired as fast as they could at the approaching American line for as long as they could until they began to run low on ammunition. Not a moment too soon, the American advance faltered, and they began to fall back in the direction from which they came, having only succeeded in losing many men killed and wounded.

Seeing they were running low on ammunition, Christof yelled over the sound of the dissipating gunfire, "Well, if the Americans didn't know we were here, they do now! They will come back, I'm sure! We need more ammo! I'm going to the rear to get more ammo before they return!"

Before Wilhelm could protest, Christof was up and out of their firing position and heading for the rear in search of more ammunition.

No sooner had Christof gotten out of sight, American artillery rounds began landing in the woods where Christof's regiment was located. For what seemed like an eternity, the world exploded around Christof and his regiment as the ground shook beneath their feet and trees exploded over their heads throughout the regiment's position.

It took Christof twice as long to return to their fighting position, considering he had to dodge incoming artillery fire. On one occasion, Christof had the air knocked out of his lungs when an artillery shell landed so close it knocked him off his feet, and he landed at the bottom of a shell crater. After regaining his senses, he was horrified to see what was left of several soldiers scattered in a gory mess at the bottom of the muddy hole.

Horrified at the gore he fell into, Christof vomited as the stench of death, blood, and the overwhelming smell of cordite assaulted his nostrils. Gathering the ammunition he dropped when he was knocked into the crater, Christof clawed his way out of the crater and scampered back toward his own fighting position.

After he dropped back into his fighting hole, Wilhelm said, "Thank God, you're back! What took you so long? I thought the artillery had gotten you!"

"You can't get rid of me that easily, my friend," Christof said as he handed Wilhelm ammunition for his rifle.

"It's a good thing you got back when you did. The sergeant came by a minute ago in between artillery strikes and said they are expecting another big push by the Americans anytime now," Wilhelm yelled.

"I'll bet they'll be coming as soon as this artillery lifts. They know we're here this time, so they will come at us faster. We need to be ready," Christof said, "make sure you're rifle is clean, so it doesn't jam, and we have hand grenades at the ready."

"Already done!" Wilhelm said, "I'll bet—"

The next thing I knew, there was a tremendous explosion near our fighting hole. That was the last thing I heard my friend say before my world went dark ...

As Lisa continued to drive, Luke said, "There's even a part in here talking to his then fiancé about his wounds and how he was in a convalescent hospital a month later outside of Berlin. Check this out!"

My dearest Anna,
Greetings from Berlin! I am writing from my hospital

bed with news. By now, you know that I was wounded in the fierce fighting near Belleau Woods in France. I am writing to you to give you an update on my condition. I am now missing the lower part of my left arm, and as such, the doctors have deemed me unfit for further military service, and I am to be discharged. Though I will carry physical scars for the rest of my life, my love for you is unwavering and will sustain me in these trying times. I pray for the time I can see your beautiful smile again soon!

    Forever Yours,

    Christof

"That is stunning!" Lisa said, "I think we've stumbled onto something amazing here."

"So do I," Luke replied in awe, "It seems like it took the better part of another month, but Christof was discharged, and he finally made it home to Anna. Even though the physical wounds to his arm were almost fully healed, it took many years for the wounds to his soul to recover. Not long after Christof made it home, he and Anna were married."

"Is that all so far?" Lisa asked.

"No, he goes on to say that, of course, the war eventually ended, and in the coming years, Germany would find its economy ruined by the terms of the armistice, and many Germans would not be able to find jobs due to the post-war economy.

With the German economy in ruins and soldiers still returning home from the now-disbanded military, Christof joined the multitudes of other German males trying to find a job. Unable to find work, Christof and Anna decided to leave Germany and immigrate to the United States, where Christof found his true calling as a lighthouse keeper. And with that new calling, Christof found the peace he had been seeking."

Lisa said, "I can't wait to dive into researching this more. It's like stepping back in time. I can almost hear the sounds of battle and see ships from around the world passing on the horizon."

"I know what you mean," Luke said, astonished as he thumbed through the rest of the journal he was holding. "At first glance, the time between the two world wars is full of mundane lighthouse stuff like different ships coming and going and a couple of run-ins with the town locals. They did not like him much because he fought for the Germans during the Great War, which I have to say is ... understandable."

As they pulled up to their small yet ample apartment, Lisa replied, "I'd have to agree. It couldn't have been easy, at least for a time."

Once the pair cleaned up and had a nice dinner, they put the journals into order by date and began the arduous task of methodically reading and transcribing every line of each journal until the history of the lighthouse, the people who lived there, and the nearby town of Smugglers Cove, all came into focus.

After a while, it became apparent that Christof wrote about everything from his time in the German Army during the war to town gossip he picked up on his runs into town to typical daily ship sightings.

As the pair delved into the journals, they soon realized that everything began to change starting in 1940, and it wouldn't be long before they found out why the journals were hidden away in the manner they were. Before long, Luke and Lisa would find themselves deeply intertwined in the lighthouse's history and solve an eighty-one-year-old murder that would forever change how the world saw the picturesque seaside town of Smugglers Cove.

1

May 1940

E ven though it was difficult at first, Christof found what he was looking for in the solitude of the lighthouse. Often, he would sit atop the massive structure, gaze out over the water, reflect on his time in the military, and write in his journal about what had brought him to this point.

Sometimes, as ships passed by at sea, Christof would look at the passing ship and wonder if his friend Wilhelm could possibly be on that ship. Despite trying, he was never able to find out what became of his friend after the artillery strike. Much of his regiment was wiped out in the coming days, and deep down, Christof knew his friend probably didn't survive the blast that took his arm, but it was still nice to think about.

Other times, he would practice his English by reading books aloud in his new language. Often, Christof would help Thomas log all the different flags they have spotted over the years or write in his many journals.

As soon as they immigrated to the United States, Christof realized that the more he wrote in English, the faster he picked it up. Many nights, After Anna went to bed, Christof would sit outside, listen to the waves crashing, and write in his journal. He wrote about everything, his upbringing in Germany, his parents, and his experiences during the war.

Christof found it especially soothing to write about his wartime experiences. The more he wrote, the less nightmares invaded his head when he slept, so he kept writing. He wrote about immigrating to the United States, starting to work at the lighthouse, and his life in general.

One day, Christof had just come down from the lighthouse after performing some routine maintenance on the lighthouse lens and doing some writing. As soon as he emerged from the lighthouse, he was greeted warmly by his ten-year-old son Thomas, who excitedly asked, "Did you see any other ships?"

Smiling at Thomas, Christof said, "No, not today. It's quiet out there right now."

"Ok," Thomas said as he ran to his room to write it down in his journal. Thomas had a list of ships and countries the ships came from, and every time he spotted a new ship or flag, he was excited all over again.

"Wash up for lunch as soon as you're done with that," Anna said as she gave Christof a peck on the lips.

"I will," Thomas said from his room.

"That goes for you, too," Anna said to Christof with a smile.

"I will, and I bet it will only take me half the time," Christof said with an evil snicker as he held up his left arm, which was missing the lower half of his forearm.

"You're bad," Anna said with a giggle.

"Yes, I know," Christof said, smiling.

A few minutes later, all three sat at the large picnic-style table and had a nice lunch of rich potato soup with onions and some leftover bacon from breakfast. On top of that, they also had freshly baked biscuits with honey.

Once they finished eating lunch, Christof said, "Thomas, help your mother clean up, and I may bring you something back when I go into town."

"Like what?" Thomas asked excitedly.

"I don't know, we'll have to see, won't we ... as long as you help your mother, that is," Christof said.

"I will!" Thomas replied, "I promise!"

"Ok, then," Christof said as he stood up from the table.

"What do you need from town?" Anna asked.

"Just some cleaning supplies for the glass up top and another journal."

"Well, I could use some more flour since you're going into town," Anna said.

"Is there anything else?" Christof asked.

"Nothing that I can think of, dear," Anna replied.

"Well, I will be leaving in a few minutes if you change your mind between now and then," Christof said.

"Okay, but I think that's all I need," Anna replied as Christof grabbed a light jacket and ensured he had his truck keys.

After slipping into his jacket, Christof said, "I shouldn't be too long, maybe an hour."

Anna walked with Christof to the front door, gave him a peck on the lips, and said, "Well, be careful."

"I will," Christof said as he walked outside to his old beat-up truck.

Christof hopped in the old truck and slammed the driver's door. He then pumped the gas pedal a few times to get the gas moving while turning the ignition at the same time. It took a moment, but the old truck's engine finally caught and came to life.

After letting the truck idle for a moment or two, he waved at Anna, who was standing in the doorway, and drove off.

Fifteen minutes later, Christof pulled into the quaint seaside town of Smugglers Cove. After driving down the main part of town, passing multiple sea captain's homes and seaside restaurants along the way, he pulled up to the general store and got out.

As Christof opened the door and stepped inside, the little bell atop the door rang as he entered with a ding, ding, to let the store owner know he had a new customer. Moments later, a middle-aged man walked out of the back room and said, "Christof... hello, my friend! How are you?"

"Hello, Joseph! I am doing well," Christof said. I just came to pick up some cleaning supplies for the lighthouse, some flour for my wife, and a new journal for me.

"Ah, I see. Well, you know where the flour and the journals are, and I have some cleaning supplies in the back that just came into the shop. Let me go get them for you. I'll be right back."

While Christof walked over to grab a bag of flour for Anna and a new journal for himself, Joseph walked into the back room to grab the cleaning supplies for Christof. After grabbing the flour and his journal, Christof walked over to the register and waited for Joseph to return.

As he stood there waiting for Joseph to come out of the back, he heard the ding, ding of the bell at the front door. Knowing quite a few people in the town, Christof instinctively turned to see if he knew who was coming in.

As soon as he turned around and saw the three men walking in and looking at him, he felt uneasy. "Ya see boys. I told you it was that German's truck out front," The man said, snickering to his buddies.

"You sure did," another man said as all three men eyed Christof.

Christof replied in his thickly accented English, "I just came for supplies. I don't want trouble."

As the three men slowly approached Christof, he turned his back to the counter, glancing around to see if there was anywhere he could escape.

One of the men eyed Christof's missing hand and asked, "What happened?"

Trying to lighten the moment, Christof smiled and replied, "I got too close to an incoming artillery shell."

Just then, Joseph, the shop owner, came out of the back room, saw what was happening, and snapped, "What's going on here? Billy! You and your brothers leave him alone!"

The man known as Billy smiled, stepped back, and said, "We're just having a little fun with Fritz there, Joseph. Settle down."

Joseph reached into the shelf under his register, pulled out a bat, and said, "His name's Christof, and if you're not going to buy something, you boys need to leave ... now."

Billy looked at his brothers Andy and Tommy and said, "That just figures. Can you believe it, boys? Old Joseph is catering to the same Germans who killed a lot of our boys in Europe!" Billy looked at Joseph and said, "Or have you forgotten?"

"No! I haven't forgotten, but I have forgiven and moved on with my life, and you need to do the same."

Billy gazed at Joseph and said, "I can't move on. I got buddies that are still buried over there in the mud where they died."

Sensing Billy's pain, Christof hesitated briefly and said, "I also lost a lot during the war. I lost my best friend in the same explosion that took my arm."

"Where?" Billy asked.

"A place called Belleau Wood. My regiment came under intense shelling, and the next thing I knew, it was a week later, and I was in the rear area."

Billy stared at Christof momentarily, then glanced at his brothers and said, "Let's get out of here, boys."

As Billy and his brothers left the store, Joseph said, "I'm sorry about that, Christof. It's been nearly twenty years since the war ended. Some people can't seem to get over it."

"I know my friend. I was one of them for a long time," Christof said.

"So, what else will you be needing?"

Christof reached down and picked up a package of candy for Thomas and said, "Just some candy for Thomas."

"Sure, no problem," Joseph replied with a smile.

After packaging Christof's items, Joseph said, "Have a good day, my friend, and ... be careful."

Christof smiled and said, "I will, and you do the same. Could you put this on my tab?"

"Consider it done ... and if you ever need to talk, you're always welcome here."

"Thank you, my friend," Christof replied, picking up his order and walking towards the door.

Christof carefully opened the door, stepped onto the sidewalk, and walked to his truck's passenger side. As he set his order in the truck, Christof felt two hands grab him from behind and spin him around violently.

Before he could say or do anything, Billy punched him in the eye and snapped, "That's for the Marines!"

Christof reeled from the punch and dropped to one knee, but before Billy or his brothers could do anything else, Joseph, who had been watching through his store's window, came storming out of his store, swinging his bat as hard as he could. "You boys, leave him alone!"

Billy and his brothers scattered and took off running down the street, hooting and hollering like they had the best time.

"Are you ok?" Thomas asked.

"Yes, thanks to you," Christof replied as he rubbed his cheek.

"Would you like me to call the sheriff?" Joseph asked, "I know it probably won't do much good, but it wouldn't hurt to report it. The Holcomb boys are a bunch of jerks."

As Christof got to his feet, he shook his head and said somberly, "No, I fear that will only make things worse. I'm just going to go back to the lighthouse."

Christof walked around the front of the old truck to the driver's side, hopped in, and slowly drove off toward the lighthouse.

2

Not long after his run-in with Billy and his brothers at the store, Christof pulled up to the lighthouse and stepped out of the truck. No sooner had he closed the driver's door than he heard Thomas come running out and excitedly say, "I helped Mother clean up like you said. What did you bring me?" Thomas noticed the swelling around Christof's eye and asked, "What's wrong with your eye?"

Ignoring Thomas' question for the moment, Christof reached into the bag of things he had just gotten in town and handed Thomas a package of candy. "It's nothing, just a little bump," Christof replied. Thomas smiled, hugged his father, and ran inside to show his mother what he had gotten.

Before the door closed behind Thomas, Christof heard him say, "Father got into a fight again, but look what he brought me."

Christof smiled and thought to himself, *he's smart. I can't get anything past him.*

Before the door even had a chance to close, Anna came bolting outside to see what Thomas meant about Christof getting in a fight again.

"What happened this time?" Anna asked.

"Just the usual bullies being bullies because I'm German. That's all," Christof replied.

Anna asked, "I thought all of that went away over time?"

"It did for quite a few years. Until Hitler came to power and started taking over countries, then it started all over again, I'm afraid."

"But that's not your fault," Anna countered.

"No, but others don't see it that way. I'm German, so around here, it's always going to be my fault, I'm afraid," Christof replied somberly as they walked inside.

As Anna walked to the kitchen and ran a rag under cool water, she asked, "Did you report it?"

"No. Joseph, the store owner, asked if I wanted to, but I told him no because I was scared it would only make matters worse."

"Here, put this on your eye," Anna said as she handed Christof the cool rag.

Christof took the rag from Anna, gently held it against his eye, and said, "Besides, you know just as well as I do any report I made would simply disappear. No ... in time, it will all fade away just as it has done in the past. What kind of father would I be if I ran to the sheriff every time something happened?"

Anna snapped, "The kind of father that sticks up for himself, that's what kind."

"You know, just like I do, my report will get lost or simply thrown away," Christof replied.

Anna gently laid her head on Christof's chest and replied, "Perhaps it won't do any good, but it will set an example for our son."

"I know, my love, but I just don't have it in me to fight anymore," Christof replied softly. He turned around, slowly walked into their bedroom, and closed the door.

After Christof went to their room, Thomas walked in and asked, "What's wrong?"

"Oh ... nothing honey, your father is just a little tired, that's all."

Anna saw Thomas thinking about something and said, "Why don't people like Father?"

Anna smiled and said, "It's not that they don't like your father. It's more like they don't like where he was born. That's all."

"That's a dumb reason not to like somebody," Thomas said.

"Yes, it is," Anna replied with a sigh.

"Will they ever like him?"

"In time, I think they will," Anna said as she gave Thomas a reassuring smile."

"THAT'S SAD," Lisa said as she listened to Luke read from the journal he was holding.

"You aren't kidding," Luke replied. I'll bet it was hard being a German immigrant and coming to the United States back then. It sounds like when he first got here, Christof was bullied, and after a time, the bullying began to fade."

"I'm thinking the same thing," Lisa said, "but when Germany started World War II, it seems to have started all over again."

"I can't wait to read the rest of these journals," Luke said. If there is some really good stuff in there, maybe we could turn this into a coffee table book and put one in each room for our guests when we finally open the bed and breakfast."

"Even if it turns out not to be that interesting, that is a great idea," Lisa said.

Before they knew it, it was nearly one thirty in the morning, so they decided to call it a night and get some sleep.

The following morning, the pair got up, and each had a cup of coffee before leaving for the thirty-minute drive to the lighthouse in the next town. Although it was cool and dreary, Luke and Lisa were excited about what the day held in store for them.

They stopped at a little mom-and-pop restaurant on the way to the lighthouse with the best biscuits. After grabbing a couple of sausage biscuits for each of them and more coffee, they drove and ate in silence for the remaining fifteen minutes.

As they pulled onto their newly purchased property, they were glad to see that the workers who had been hired to renovate the property were already there and beginning to pick up right where they had left off. Luke and Lisa found the project manager and, after a short conversation, found out that if all went smoothly, they would be finished with all the renovations and ready for their walkthrough in a little over a week.

The project manager, a tall and friendly older man named Joe, and his contractor Shawn walked Luke and Lisa through the property, showing them each room in the main house attached to the lighthouse, which had already been completely renovated.

After seeing what had been done and what still needed to be done, Joe said, "I'm going to need color swatches soon so my guys can get started painting in the rooms that have already been finished."

"That's the plan for today. As soon as the stores open around here, we will be looking for paint, furniture, and decorations," Lisa said with a smile, "This is going to be fun!"

Luke looked at Joe a little less enthused and said, "Oh ... boy. Joe, are you sure you don't need any help around here, like scraping seagull shit off something that needs to be painted? Anything to get me out of going shopping," Luke pleaded.

Joe laughed, smiled, and said, "Sorry, but nope. We have it all handled. You and Lisa run along and have fun."

Luke rolled his eyes playfully and said, "Gee, thanks, buddy."

Lisa playfully smacked Luke and said, "Let's go before you get yourself into trouble, mister."

The pair drove into town and spent the next hour or more looking at different paint swatches and color schemes. While they were looking at the different colors, an older man walked up and said, "Hi, folks. Can I help you with something?"

"We're just picking out colors for our house, that's all. There are way too many colors to choose from these days," Lisa said with a smile.

"Tell me about it," the man said, "There are dozens of colors and hundreds of different shades and hues on top of that. My name is Lewis, and I am the owner," he said as he introduced himself.

"Shaking hands with the owner, Luke said, "Nice to meet you. I'm Luke Wolf, and this is my wife, Lisa."

Taking in every word of what the newcomers to his store said, Lewis asked, "Are you the two that are renovating the lighthouse and turning it into a bed and breakfast?"

"Yes, we are. How did you know about that?" Lisa asked.

"Oh, you might say it's the talk of the town," Lewis replied.

"What do you mean?" Luke asked.

Lewis thought momentarily and said, "Well ... you didn't hear this from me, but there are folks in this town that are none too happy about you fixing up the old lighthouse and moving in."

"Why's that?" Lisa asked, "We don't even know anybody here. What have we done?"

"You haven't done anything. It's just that folks were hoping to leave the past in the past. They're scared that you folks moving in, and renovating will only stir up old feelings that people around here had rather not stir up again."

"I don't understand," Luke said.

"Your last name is Wolf. Correct?"

"Yes," Luke acknowledged.

"So, I guess it's no stretch of the imagination to assume your family has been living there and running the lighthouse since World War I. Right?"

"More or less," Luke replied warily.

"Do you know any of your family's past at the lighthouse?" Lewis asked.

"Just the basics," Luke conceded.

"Well, let's say there's a lot of history at that old lighthouse and let's just leave it at that. Shall we?"

"Wait, you can't just leave us hanging like that," Lisa exclaimed.

Lewis exhaled deeply and replied, "Look, folks, you two seem to be good, decent people. It's nothing against you personally. Really, it's not. It's simply that some folks around Smugglers Cove were really hoping for ... a different family. That's all."

Luke replied, "You mean one that doesn't have my last name. Don't you?"

"Honestly ... yes. It makes no difference to me, but I think certain townsfolk won't be too happy to know that the Wolf family still owns the lighthouse."

"You still haven't said why, though," Lisa replied.

Lewis replied, "Nope, I didn't, and I'm not going to."

Before they could ask anything else, another customer walked in. Lewis said, "Take all the time you need, folks, but another customer needs my help." With that, Lewis turned and abruptly walked off to help the other customer that had just walked in.

Luke glanced at Lisa and said, "That was strange."

"Strange indeed," Lisa replied. "Maybe buying some paint would loosen him up a little bit."

"That is a good idea, my dear," Luke replied with a wink, "let's get to picking out colors."

The pair stood there for another thirty minutes, picking out several colors. Once they decided which color was going in each room, they headed to the front with the swatches. On the way out, Lewis asked, "Did you find what you needed?"

"We sure did. We picked out several different colors. We will take the swatches and give them to our project manager so they can determine how much of each color we need."

"Fantastic. I'll be waiting for the order. Do you need anything else?"

Lisa thought momentarily and asked, "Are there any antique stores around or anything like that?"

Lewis replied with a smile and said, "There sure are. If you go down the block, turn right, then a half a mile or so, you'll see Sunset Road. Turn right again, and you'll see several antique stores on both sides of the road." Lewis paused a moment and said, "You will also find the town library and historical center on the same street. It's in an old house. You might stop in there and have a look around, too."

"Thank you for the information," Luke said cheerfully as he and Lisa left the paint store and returned to their car.

When they got in their car, Luke asked, "What was that about? Do you think Lewis was hinting that we should go have a look around the library?"

"I think that's exactly what he was doing," Lisa replied.

"So, whatcha wanna do first?" Luke asked.

Lisa thought momentarily and replied, "Lewis has my curiosity up now. Let's go to the library and historical center."

Luke smiled and said, "I was hoping you would say that."

Following Lewis's directions, Luke and Lisa quickly found the historical center and library, parked, and went inside. As soon as they walked in, they were greeted warmly by an older lady with greying hair and large, wide glasses seated behind a counter. "Hello! My name is Ruth. I'm the town librarian and historian. What brings you two in today?"

Lisa replied, "This is Luke, and I'm Lisa. We're new to the area, and we were buying paint nearby, and the owner suggested we come in and have a look around."

"Ah, that's great. Always good to see younger couples moving into the area. What part of town did you move to?"

"Well, we didn't exactly move into town," Luke replied, "we're moving into the lighthouse."

"Oh ... I see. You must be the Wolfs," Ruth said, her body language changing once she realized who she was talking to. "Feel free to look around; I'll be right here if you need anything. It's primarily books on the upper floor and the town's history here on the first floor."

Sensing the chill in the room and suddenly feeling uncomfortable, Lisa made eye contact with Luke and said, "We will."

The duo began slowly looking around in the different rooms and display cases scattered around. There were also old, framed newspapers on the walls and pictures of old ships on the horizon. Everywhere you looked, there was something on display. As Luke and Lisa slowly walked around, they entered a smaller room near the back of the house, and they were amazed to see an old black-and-white picture of the lighthouse.

"Look at that old picture," Luke exclaimed.

As they walked up to take a closer look at the picture, Lisa pointed out something odd. She saw where an X had been drawn on the actual picture under the glass. "Wonder what the X is for on the picture?" Lisa asked aloud, knowing that it must have also been going through Luke's mind.

"Maybe Ruth at the front desk knows," Luke replied, "let's find out."

They walked over to the front, where the woman sat quietly, and Luke said, "Excuse me, but we have a question."

"What can I help you with?" The woman answered monotoned without looking up.

Luke said, "Near the back, there's an old, framed photo of the lighthouse hanging on the wall."

"I'm familiar with it," the woman said. "What would you like to know about it?"

"Do you know why an X is marked off to the side on the picture? It's hard to tell from the picture, but it kinda looks like someone marked a location near the beach."

"I know the picture," the woman replied smugly, "that X is the approximate location of where poor Sarah Harper's body was found."

"What happened? Did she drown? Lisa asked.

"No," the woman replied without looking up from what she was doing. "She was murdered back in 1942 ... repeatedly stabbed with a knife."

"That's terrible," Lisa replied, trying to make small talk and get some information from the woman. "I hope they caught the person who did it."

"No. At the time, the sheriff never found out who did it. Of course, he investigated it, but there wasn't much to go on. There wasn't much around there then ... except for the lighthouse."

"What's that supposed to mean?" Luke asked.

The woman stopped what she was doing, looked up at Luke and Lisa, and said, "It was before my time, but rumor around the town was that someone nearby did it ... possibly from the lighthouse."

"You mean someone from my family. Don't you?" Luke replied sternly.

"That was the rumor back then, and I hate to say it, but there are still those around today who think that somebody in the Wolf family was to blame for the murder, among other things."

"What sort of ... other things?" Luke asked, getting irritated at the woman.

"They were rumors mostly," Ruth replied.

Luke pressed more and said, "Like what?"

"As soon as the war started, there was a siting of a stranger in town that seemingly appeared overnight then just as quickly disappeared. Some folks thought Christof Wolf helped a German spy come ashore from a U-boat off the coast. One fella who was shot and killed not far from here supposedly turned out to be an actual German spy. Nobody found out where he came from or how he got here."

Lisa looked at Luke and asked, "Have you ever heard of this before?"

"No, I've never heard of this part of the family lore before," Luke admitted, "It does explain a lot, though."

"Like what?" Lisa asked.

"Just some things, like why nobody likes to talk about what happened to Christof or the supposed 'bad luck' the family seems to have had in the past. That's okay, though. I think I know where we might be able to find the answers," Luke said with a devious smile.

"So do I!" Lisa replied excitedly. I'll bet it could be in the journals we found! Are you about ready to continue our excursion?" Lisa asked.

"Sure, let's go," Luke replied, "thanks for all of your help."

"Wait, what journals?" Ruth asked, trying not to sound excited.

Lisa started to reply, but Luke grabbed her hand as if to stop her and said, "Oh, nothing really. We just found some old journals during the renovations. So far, there's nothing interesting in them, and most of it is unreadable. Thanks again for the help."

"You're welcome and I'd love to see the journals sometime when you get a chance. Where are you two off to now?" Ruth asked somewhat innocently.

"Oh, we're going to hit some of the antique stores around here to see what we can find for the lighthouse before we head back," Lisa said.

Luke reiterated, "We will bring them by some time, but as I said, they are mostly unreadable."

"Well, that's a shame. I always love learning about the town's history, so if there's anything good in there, I'm always here. There are several good stores around here. I imagine you'll find something you like. If you're hungry there's also a nice café down from there too." Ruth said.

Before turning to leave, Luke caught sight of another photo on Ruth's desk. It showed an infant lying down, covered in a blanket that resembled the Baby Ruth candy bar. Luke pointed at the picture and said, "I gotta ask. What's with the picture of the baby under the blanket?"

Ruth replied, "Oh, that's my daughter. When she was little, I put her in all sorts of Baby Ruth candy bar clothes. To this day, she still hates that candy bar."

Luke and Lisa left the library and historical center. As they walked down the sidewalk toward the car, Luke glanced over his shoulder at the posted closing time in case they needed to return. Looking back, he could see Ruth already on the phone calling somebody.

"That old lady is already on the phone. I'll bet she couldn't wait for us to leave so she could call and start spreading the word about who just came in and what we found. I wish you hadn't said anything to her about the journals," Luke replied.

Lisa said, "I'm sorry, I just got caught up in the moment. Anyway, bring on the antique stores!"

"Oh ... yay!" Luke replied sarcastically.

～

NOT FAR AWAY AT the Sheriff's office, Sheriff Eddie Baxter was at his desk doing paperwork when the phone on his desk rang. Picking it up on the second ring, the sheriff said, "Sheriff Baxter."

He instantly recognized the raspy voice as she blurted, "Sheriff, I just had a couple in here you may want to know about."

"Well, hello to you too, Ruth. Who was that?"

"The new couple that bought the lighthouse. That's who," Ruth shot back.

"Were they just looking around or what?"

"Yeah, they were looking around and said they were going to go antique shopping for the lighthouse, but that's not all!"

"Okay, okay, settle down before you blow a vein or something, Ruth. What else is there?"

Ruth replied, "They were just looking around, but then they saw the old picture of the lighthouse and the beach and started asking questions about it."

"What sort of questions?" Sheriff Baxter asked.

"They wanted to know what the X meant marked on the photo and before—"

Baxter interrupted Ruth mid-sentence and snapped, "What did you tell them?"

"I'm sorry, but before I knew it, I had told them about the Harper girl's murder."

"You did what?" Baxter nearly shouted into the phone.

"I'm sorry but I changed the subject real quick. I started telling them about the German spy rumor, which piqued their interest more than the murder."

"Damn it, Ruth," Sheriff Baxter snapped. "Did they say where they were going after that?"

"No, I just told them where the closest antique stores were. They shouldn't be hard to find. If you want to introduce yourself to them."

"I just may do that." Sheriff Baxter replied.

"There is one curious thing, though," Ruth said.

"What's that?"

Ruth said, "The wife ... I think she said her name was Lisa;

anyway, she let it slip that they had found some journals during the renovations."

"Really now?" Baxter asked curiously. "Did they say what was in them?"

"Not really. The husband stepped in and said the journals were not readable, but I could tell that the wife was caught off guard by his answer."

"Okay, thanks," Baxter said before hanging up, "but don't go blabbing anymore to those two about the murder. Understand?"

"I understand," Ruth replied.

After hanging up the phone, Sheriff Baxter sat back in his chair and said, "Shit."

3

After visiting two antique stores and a trinket store, Luke and Lisa found a few things for the lighthouse and drove down the street to the last store they planned on hitting that day.

After parking and walking inside, they were greeted warmly by a young girl. She told them to take their time looking around and to let her know if there was anything she could do. They stayed in the store for about twenty minutes, bought a few items, and went to pay.

While paying for the items, Lisa asked if there were any places around to eat lunch. The young girl told them there was a good café not far away and gave them directions on how to get there. They thanked the young girl and a few minutes later found themselves pulling up to the small café, which had seating inside or outside in a small area beside the sidewalk.

Once they checked in with the hostess, they opted to sit outside since the weather was nice. In a few minutes, the waitress came out, took their drink order, and said she would return to take their lunch order. They looked over the menu and made small talk for a few minutes, and when the waitress returned, they both opted for the turkey club sandwich and fries.

While they were sitting there waiting for their food, they noticed a sheriff's car slowly driving past and pulling into the parking area for the café. "This must be a good place if the sheriff eats here," Luke replied.

"Yeah, either that or it's the only place around," Lisa smirked.

A few minutes later, an older sheriff walked up the sidewalk towards the café. As he walked up, he stopped and talked to several people he obviously knew and then walked over to the table where Luke and Lisa were sitting, "Good afternoon," he said with a smile.

Luke and Lisa smiled, and both replied, "Hello. How are you?"

"I'm doing fine," the sheriff replied, "I'm Sheriff Eddie Baxter. I know most folks around here and don't believe I know you. Are you passing through?"

Luke replied, "Not exactly. We live in the next town over, but we just bought the lighthouse and are renovating it to become a bed and breakfast. When the renovations are finished, we will be living here full-time."

"I see, so that would make you the Wolfs, then?" Sheriff Baxter replied.

"That would be us," Luke replied as he extended his hand to shake hands with the sheriff, "I'm Luke, and this is my wife, Lisa."

Shaking hands with Luke, the sheriff replied, "Well, the townsfolk are glad to see that the property is being put to good use ... even if it is by the same family."

"What does that mean?" Lisa asked.

"What I mean is, there are those that were hoping for ... new owners, that's all," the sheriff replied.

"Well, there are new owners—us," Luke said as he stared at the sheriff.

"So, it would seem," Sheriff Baxter replied as the waitress returned with their food, "you have a good lunch," the sheriff replied as he walked inside.

"You too," Luke said as the sheriff walked off.

"What was that about?" Lisa asked.

"Somehow, I get the distinct feeling that certain people in this town still don't like the Wolf family name," Luke replied.

"I'm starting to get the same feeling," Lisa said, uneasy. "What's going on around here?"

Luke took a bite of his sandwich, then said, "I don't know, but I have a feeling I know where we might find the answers."

"So do I," Lisa said excitedly, "In the journals."

"Exactly," Luke replied, "let's finish here, then take our loot back to the lighthouse."

Lisa replied, "After that, we can check in with the contractor and head back home to dive into the journals more. Hopefully, we can at least get some insight from Christof's perspective."

"My sentiments exactly. Luke replied.

After finishing their meal and paying, Luke and Lisa returned to their car and went back through the small seaside town toward the lighthouse. As they drove through the center of town, they made a few more stops at some interesting-looking places, and then Lisa said, "I sure would like a cup of coffee."

"That actually sounds good," Luke replied, "and maybe a Danish too."

About that time, Lisa said excitedly, "Look, a coffee shop! Let's stop!"

Luke pulled to the curb and read the sign aloud, "Riaha's Coffee and Pastries."

"Looks like a neat little place," Lisa said, hopeful.

"Sure does. Let's give it a shot," Luke replied, "We aren't on a time schedule or anything."

After parking, both hopped out and walked into the quaint coffee shop. They saw a young woman look up from behind the counter as they entered. Glancing around the coffee shop, several patrons were chatting or taking advantage of the free Wi-Fi and doing work on their computers.

On every wall of the shop were either beautiful paintings or photos of the surrounding area, including a few of their lighthouse. They walked up to the counter and were greeted warmly by an attractive young woman with a beautiful mocha complexion and shoulder-length locks pulled up off her shoulders with a hair tie.

"Hi! My name's Riaha, welcome to my coffee shop," the young woman said, flashing a beautiful smile. "What can I get you?"

"Two coffees, both with a splash of cream and two cheese danishes," Luke said.

"I got you," the young lady replied, "coming right up."

As she fixed their orders, Riaha said, "Are you guys passing through, or are you new to the area?"

"We're new to the area. We're renovating the lighthouse into a bed and breakfast," Luke replied.

"Fantastic!" Riaha replied, "Well, this is my coffee shop, and I'm proud to say it's a local hangout. Much of the town gossip has been spread in these walls."

"Well, I'm Lisa, and this is my husband, Luke Wolf. It is very nice to meet you too, Riaha," Lisa said.

"It's nice to meet you both as well. You guys can sit anywhere you like, and I'll bring your order over to you when it's ready," Riaha said with a warm and cheerful smile.

Luke and Lisa picked out a table for two near a window by the front of the shop so they could see the town and took a seat. "So, what do you think of the town?" Luke asked.

"I think it's a charming and picturesque town. There aren't many lodging options around, so I really think once the renovations are complete, we won't have any trouble keeping it going," Lisa replied.

"Yeah, especially with the views of the ocean, the antique stores, and now this coffee shop. I think we will do great!" Luke said excitedly.

A moment or two later, Riaha came to their table with their orders and cheerfully said, "Here you go, two coffees, both with a splash of cream, and two cheese danishes. Is there anything else I can get for you?"

Luke sipped the steaming coffee and said, "I think we're good. Man! That's good coffee."

Riah replied, "It's fair trade and Rainforest Alliance certified. I sell several different types of coffee, but this is my favorite."

"I can see why," Lisa said, smiling as she sipped the smooth-tasting coffee.

Riaha said, "I'll leave you two in peace. Enjoy."

As she turned to leave, Luke said, "Just a moment, I have a question for you."

"Sure. What's that?" Riaha asked.

"What do you think of the sheriff?"

"He's not bad," Riaha replied. "The ex-sheriff is the one that always gave me the creeps. Why do you ask?"

Luke cautiously told Riaha what had happened on their excursion into town after leaving the historical center and how the sheriff happened to show up at the same place the older lady from the historical center suggested they eat.

When Riaha heard what Luke said, she giggled and said, "I'm not surprised. That's Ruth. She and the Baxters are tight. I'm not sure how or why unless they're related somehow. There's no doubt, though, that the first thing she did when you left was to call the sheriff. Not to get you in trouble or anything ... so that he could accidentally bump into you and introduce himself."

"We still don't get why, though," Lisa said.

"He always likes to introduce himself to newcomers into town, that's all."

"Makes sense," Luke replied.

Riaha said, "Well, I have some work to do behind the counter, so I'll leave you two alone and let you enjoy your coffees and danishes."

After the young coffee shop owner walked off, Luke said, "I like this place. The atmosphere is nice."

"So do I," Lisa replied, "this could be a place we recommend to our guests when they're looking for places to go in town."

After the pair finished their coffee and danishes, they went to the counter to pay their bill. Riaha quickly scribbled something on a piece of receipt paper and said, "Here's your receipt."

"You can trash it," Luke said, smiling, "I don't need it."

Riaha looked directly into Luke's eyes and said, "You should always check your receipt. You never know."

"I'll do that," Luke replied with a smile, "thank you."

As Luke and Lisa turned for the front door, they heard Riaha say cheerfully, "Come back to see me anytime!"

"Oh, don't worry. I think we'll be regulars here. Lisa replied with a smile, "Coffee is my drink of choice!"

"We're going to be seeing a lot of each other," Luke said, giggling as they walked out.

As they hopped into their car, Luke thought about what Riaha had said and glanced at the folded receipt she had given him. Lisa watched while he unfolded the receipt, then saw his eyes widen. "What is it?"

Luke handed her the receipt and saw where Riaha had written at the bottom, *not everyone is what they seem*. "That's not creepy or anything. What in the hell is that supposed to mean?" Lisa asked.

"I don't know, but evidently, she didn't feel comfortable enough to say it aloud with the people that were in there." Luke replied, "Let's head back. We need to unload the loot we picked up, check in with Joe and Shawn, and start heading home."

Fifteen minutes after retracing their path through town, Luke and Lisa made it back to the lighthouse in time to talk to the project manager for a few minutes. All three went over what still needed to be done and what was finished as the pair unloaded their finds from the local antique stores.

Once that was done, Luke and Lisa gave the project manager the paint swatches they had picked and walked through the house to show him which color was going in each room. The pair stayed with the project manager for another thirty minutes, and then Lisa asked the question they were dying to ask, "So, when do you think we can move in?"

Joe pushed his hat on his head a little, looked at the ground for a moment, and said, "Depends on you two, I guess. The master bedroom and bathroom are done. Technically speaking, you could move in anytime. We have minor things in each of the other rooms, like trim work and things. The biggest thing left is painting. If you can manage the paint smell, there's no reason why you couldn't start moving into the master bedroom tomorrow if you really wanted to."

Lisa smiled and said, "We need to get going because I think we have some packing to do!"

Luke replied, "We sure do."

"Oh, by the way, there is something I've meant to tell you," Joe said. "While we were working in the lantern room, Shawn found a recess in the wall when we were repairing one of the sills. There was nothing there, of course, but you could tell that it had been used for something in the past. Whether it was simply used for storage or for hiding something, we don't know for sure, but the way it was constructed and how it was made level with the wall, I'd say it was a hiding spot for something."

"Is it still there?" Lisa asked.

"Oh, yes, Shawn made a few repairs to it, but it's still there just as it was. The next time you go up there, check it out. It's a neat little piece of the past."

"Thank you for telling us. We will check it out when we go up," Luke replied.

Joe continued, "When you enter the lantern room, it's straight across on the right. Now that there's new paint up there, it's easier to see than when we started."

"Thank you for telling us," Lisa said excitedly, "We will have to look at it the next time we're up there."

AFTER LEAVING the lighthouse and driving to their apartment, Lisa asked, "So, what do you think of how some people in the town have acted? People can't still think your ancestor had something to do with that girl's murder. Can they? I've heard about small-town drama before, but this is on a whole new level."

Luke thought for a moment and replied, "I have no idea. I wouldn't think people would hold a grudge this long, but I really don't know. I know one thing, though. I want to go back and read Christof's journals some more. I'll be willing to bet the answer is in there."

"Do you know what happened to Christof?" Lisa asked.

"Yes ... and no," Luke replied.

"Um, what?" Lisa asked, confused.

"As the story goes, one morning, Christof was found on the ground dead at the base of the lighthouse by Anna. When she realized he wasn't in bed, Anna checked the house and couldn't find him, so she started looking around, and that's when she found him."

"That's terrible! Does anybody know what happened?" Lisa asked.

"Not really. Depending on who you talk to, some say Christof fell, but some, especially in the town, say he jumped."

"I don't believe that," Lisa replied, "he was a survivor. He would not have jumped and left his family behind to carry on without him."

Luke replied, "I agree. Most of the family do not believe he jumped. Most of the family believes he either slipped, which I personally doubt, or ... he was pushed."

"When was this?" Lisa asked.

Luke thought for a moment and said, "Somewhere right around 1955. Why do you ask?"

"No reason, just trying to get it straight in my head. So, Christof died ten years after the end of World War II."

"Correct," Luke said.

"So, it seems highly unlikely that he slipped and fell to his death off a lighthouse he had been working at for the past thirty years," Lisa said.

"Also correct," Luke replied, "which is why I'm not so sure I really believe either one."

"So, what do you believe?"

Luke said, "Well, growing up in the family, nobody would say it. I think nobody wanted to believe it, but I tend to think that he was pushed."

"Pushed!" Lisa repeated, "Why do you think that?"

"Yep. There's no proof or anything ... just a feeling."

"Why would he have been pushed?" Lisa asked flabbergasted.

"I don't know. There are so many things that happened in my family's past. It wouldn't surprise me, though," Luke replied, "also there's one other thing I kinda ... didn't tell you."

"Which is what?" Lisa asked.

Luke paused a moment and said, "Now, don't let this freak you out, but some say ... he's still here."

"I'm sorry. What?" Lisa asked wild-eyed.

"Some people have claimed in the past they had seen—"

"Seen what exactly," Lisa interjected.

"His ... ghost," Luke said, as he cringed, awaiting Lisa's response.

"When in the hell were you going to tell me?" Lisa snapped.

Luke downplayed the whole ghost rumor by saying, "There's no proof or anything, just what some people have claimed."

"Well, maybe it's a good thing we found those journals then," Lisa said. Maybe there's a clue in there, or it could be the answer to everything."

"One could only wish," Luke replied, "I'm kinda scared to know the truth, though."

"Why?" Lisa asked as she heard the pain in his voice.

"So many unknowns, the murder of that girl on the beach, Christof's death, the family trust, not to mention the car crash that took my parents."

"You know the car crash was an accident. There was nothing nefarious about it at all. Your dad had a heart attack behind the wheel and ran off the road, which is how your mom died. And what about the family trust?"

"It's always been a mystery as to where the money came from," Luke said, "nobody seems to know the truth behind it. Lighthouse keepers didn't make much money, so how could Christof save so much?"

"Don't look a gift horse in the mouth," Lisa replied, "If it weren't for your family's trust, we wouldn't be able to do this."

"I know," Luke replied, "it's just that my family's history is not the greatest around."

Lisa reached over, patted him on the leg, and said, "Well, we're going to change that starting with us."

"I hope so," Luke replied.

Lisa said, "We will. Now, let's go back to the apartment and look at the journals to see what we can find."

After safely making it home and settling in for the night, Luke and Lisa turned on the lights on each of their nightstands and got ready to read more of the journals. Luke carefully turned the page to where they had left off while Lisa opened the Word document where she was transcribing everything while Luke read.

Before long, they were again drifting back in time to another era, several lifetimes ago.

4

Mid-December 1941

One day, as Christof came down from the lighthouse doing routine maintenance, Anna was waiting for him at the base of the mammoth staircase, saying, "Perfect timing. A car just turned off the road and is pulling up now."

"Who is it?" Christof asked.

"I don't know," Anna replied, "but we will find out soon enough."

Shortly, a middle-aged man with a full beard and wire-rimmed glasses stepped out of the car that pulled up to the house beside Christof's old truck.

"Can I help you?" Christof asked as the gentleman approached Christof.

The man removed the simple hat he was wearing, held it by his side, and asked, "Perhaps. I am looking for Christof Wolf. I'm told he may run this lighthouse. Do you know where I can find him?"

Immediately, Christof and Anna recognized a slight Germanic accent. They exchanged glances at one another, and then Christof said, "I am the man you seek. What do you want?"

The man replied, "My name is Hans Dasch, and I was instructed to make contact with you with a ... business proposition."

"What sort of business proposition?" Christof asked.

The man looked around momentarily and said, "This is not the sort of thing that should be discussed outside in the open. Do you have a place where we can sit and discuss matters?"

Christof thought a moment and then said, "Yes, of course, follow me." Christof and Anna led the newcomer into the dining room off the kitchen, and the three sat at the table. No sooner had the three sat down than Thomas walked in.

The man started to say something to Thomas, but before he could, Christof said, "Thomas, I saw some masts off in the distance. Why don't you go up top and see what you can see?"

Thomas' eyes widened with excitement, and he replied, "Ok! And I know I'll be careful!"

After Thomas ran out, the three sat in awkward silence for a moment. Finally, Christof asked the man who identified himself as Hans, "What do you really want?"

Ignoring Christof momentarily, the man looked at Anna and said, "I'm terribly sorry, but I've come quite a long way. Might I trouble you for a glass of water?"

Anna stared at the man for a moment, then said, "I suppose." After she got up and walked into the kitchen, the somewhat mysterious man said, "As I've said, I've come a long way to offer you a business proposition."

"And what sort of proposition is it?"

Anna walked back in and sat a glass of water down in front of the man who picked it up, took several large gulps, and sat it back down, "Thank you," Hans said.

Anna simply nodded her head as she took a seat beside Christof. When she was settled, Hans began, "I was sent ... from Germany to make contact with certain individuals who may be in a position to help the Reich should it be needed."

Almost immediately, Christof sternly said, "I'm not interested! I left Germany years ago for the United States, and I'm not going to do anything that could get us kicked out of the country or have us arrested for aiding Germany."

"I completely understand," Hans replied, "but all we're looking for is a little cooperation on your part. You will never even have to leave your lighthouse, and of course, we will pay you for your effort."

"The answer is still no," Christof replied defiantly.

The mysterious man known as Hans took a deep breath and said, "I really hoped you would say yes. I didn't want to have to do this." Anna and Christof watched cautiously as Hans reached into a pocket, pulled out a folded piece of paper, and slid it across the table to Christof.

Christof unfolded the paper and saw two lists of names. One list included members of Christof's family, and the other included members of Anna's family. Hans took a moment to let them read the list of names and then said, "If you choose not to help the Reich, every single person on that paper will be sentenced to either a labor camp ... or worse."

Christof and Anna looked at one another, completely stunned. Christof quickly stood and, with his one good arm, reached for the knife he kept sheathed on his side.

"I wouldn't do that," Hans replied matter-of-factly, "If for some reason I don't return, the Reich will simply send another person to take my place. And if that person should also fail to return, every person on that list will be ... relocated."

Finally, after being so shocked he couldn't speak, Christof lowered his head, then looked at Anna and asked, "What choice do we have?"

Still in shock, Anna could only nod in agreement.

"What will I have to do?" Christof asked, saddened.

The man smiled devilishly and replied, "Nothing dangerous or anything of that nature, I assure you. The Reich has a different plan in store for you."

Christof stared at the man named Hans, but he seriously doubted that was his real name. "What is it, then?"

"You are uniquely suited to help agents come ashore should the situation arise," Hans replied, "In fact, that's all we want you to do. Your lighthouse is to be a landing spot for our agents in the future. All you will have to do is help them get ashore and possibly give them a warm meal and a safe place to spend the night when they come ashore before they move off on their missions."

Christof stood up and began pacing back and forth, taking in everything the man named Hans had said. Then he replied, "How will I know when this is to happen?"

"Two nights before someone is to come ashore, you will receive a telegram that simply says *"Greetings from home"* written on it. You are to help your visitor come ashore, and once he's gone, you are to carry on as if nothing happened."

Christof stopped pacing and looked at Anna, who gave him a nearly imperceptible nod. Finally, Christof took a deep breath and said, "It will be as you say."

The mysterious man smiled and said, "Excellent! My bosses will be most pleased. As we discussed, you will also be paid a fee of one hundred dollars for your time and effort in helping our friend come ashore."

"That will be little comfort when I'm sitting in jail if I get caught," Christof snapped.

Hans got up and started for the door. Once he reached the door, he turned and said, "If someone comes around asking questions, all you did was save someone from drowning, and they ran off. Who knows, the Fuhrer may not even require your services, but we must be ready ... just in case."

With that, the mysterious man returned to his car and slowly drove off.

~

LUKE SAT IN BED, stunned at what he had just read. "I can't believe what I just read! It was true! My Great-Grandfather was a Nazi sympathizer."

"I'm not so sure about that," Lisa replied, "The way this reads, he was not a willing participant. He was, for the most part, blackmailed into helping."

Luke huffed and said dejectedly, "Yeah, but since this turned out to be true ... what if he really did kill that girl on the beach? And did you catch the part about the knife on Christof's side? Remember what the woman said at the historical center about how the woman was killed? She was stabbed."

Lisa said, "Yes, I remember, but that doesn't mean much. All it really means is that he carried a knife. That's a long way from saying he killed that girl. Why don't you stop reading for tonight? We have much to do in the next day or two, especially since we can move into the master bedroom now."

"You know I'm not going to be able to sleep now. Don't you?" Luke said, "This is going to be on my mind all night," he said as he gently laid the journal on his nightstand and turned off his lamp.

"I know," Lisa replied as she sat her laptop on the nightstand and turned her lamp off, "but you better because we have a lot to do tomorrow."

The following morning, after a restless night's sleep, the pair got up, made breakfast in their apartment, and rented a box truck to pack their bedroom and hopefully spend their first night in the lighthouse.

After picking up the box truck, Luke and Lisa returned to their apartment and began taking apart their bed and moving a few of the boxes they had already packed into the truck. They spent the next two hours packing and moving their bedroom and bathroom contents into the truck, hoping they could spend their first night at the lighthouse tonight.

One of the last things they packed was the newly found journals. Luke and Lisa took extra care of them, carefully wrapping them so they would not get damaged during the move. Then, once the journals were packed up, Luke put them in the front of the cab for the ride back to the lighthouse to ensure nothing happened to them.

Even though they still had plenty of room in the truck, Luke and Lisa stopped with just their bedroom and bathroom since they were the only rooms ready at the lighthouse. They decided to move one room at a time as the rooms were finished at the lighthouse so they would not get overwhelmed trying to move their entire apartment at the same time.

Once they finished packing their bedroom furniture and were on their way to the lighthouse, Lisa said, "You're pretty quiet over there. What's wrong?"

"Oh, nothing really. I was just thinking about what we discovered in the journal last night. Some of the townsfolk seemed to be on the right track."

"Meaning what?" Lisa asked.

"If they were right about Christof helping the Germans during World War II, they could have been right about him killing that girl, too," Luke replied dejectedly.

"I'm not so sure about that. For one thing, according to the journal, Christof was essentially blackmailed into helping the Germans by this mysterious Hans guy, and that is a long way from murdering someone for no apparent reason."

"I know, but I still can't stop thinking about it," Luke replied.

"Well, I think that the answer is somewhere in this box at my feet," Lisa replied as she pointed at the box of journals.

"I hope so," Luke replied, "after we get unloaded, let's get cleaned up and go into town to grab a cup of coffee at Riaha's."

"I like the sound of that," Lisa replied, smiling.

After spending the next several hours moving, and checking in with the project manager, they found that they were at a good stopping point and decided to get cleaned up for a coffee run. Once they had cleaned up, they took the box truck they rented, and drove it to Riaha's Coffee Shop.

Pulling up a few minutes later, Riaha was behind the counter and looked up when she heard the door open, "Hi guys! How are you doing today?"

Luke replied, "Man, we're tired. We've been moving and just finished for the day."

Lisa said, "Yep, we've worked so hard today that we thought we would treat ourselves."

"Sounds good," Riaha replied with her usual pretty smile and friendly demeanor. "What can I get for you today?"

"What do you recommend?" Luke asked.

"I have a new Columbian Blonde coffee that's nice and light. It's a good choice for this time of day," Riaha said.

"That sounds perfect," Luke and Lisa agreed. "And two of your cheese Danishes, too," Lisa added.

Riaha smiled and said, "I got you. Have a seat anywhere you like, and I will be right over with your order."

Luke and Lisa picked a corner table out of the way, sat down, and waited for their order. While they were waiting, "Lisa said monotoned, "I hurt all over. Even my hair hurts."

Luke could not help but giggle at Lisa and then said, "This is only the beginning, sweetie."

"I know, I know," Lisa said, "this is the last time I am ever moving. The next time I have to move, it will either be to a nursing home or a grave."

"I know what you mean," Luke said, smiling. I, for one, have no intention of ever moving again, so this is it for us."

Luke glanced at Riaha behind the counter and asked, "I wonder what she meant when she slipped us that note the last time we were in here."

"I'm not sure. If this place is a local hangout, there's no telling what she's heard," Lisa replied.

"Let's ask," Luke suggested.

Lisa shot back, "It couldn't hurt. Here's your chance. She's coming over now."

A moment later, Riaha walked over to their table with their order, sat it down, and asked, "Can I get you guys anything else?"

Luke replied, "We're good, but I do have a question for you, though."

"What's that?" Riaha asked.

"What was with the note you wrote on our receipt last time we were in here?"

Riaha glanced around, and even though there were only one or two people in the shop then, she lowered her voice and said, "Just know, people are already talking about the new owners of the lighthouse, and some aren't happy about it."

"I don't get why, though," Luke replied. "Does it have something to do with my ancestors being from Germany, or the rumors about Christof Wolf helping a spy come ashore in World War II, or maybe something with the murdered girl? You have to narrow it down a little for us."

Riaha said, "Look, I don't really know, but I can tell you that I've lived here for the past five years, and the talk has always been about the murdered girl Sarah Harper."

"I don't get it, though," Luke replied, "from what I've heard, that girl was killed over eighty years ago. How can the town still be hung up on that, considering everything that's happened over the past eighty years?"

Riaha lowered her voice and said, "You did not hear this from me, but there have always been whispers in town that maybe, just maybe, she didn't die like everyone thinks."

Luke looked shocked and asked, "What do you mean?"

"I'm not sure. All I know is that, from talking to different people here over the years, everybody has their own opinion, and it's apparently not what they were told. Some were hoping for new lighthouse owners because they thought the past would finally be left in the past."

"So, it sounds like it's not necessarily in the past," Lisa said.

"I think it's a regular Peyton Place around here," Riaha said.

As Riaha started to say something else, she heard the front door of her shop open. All three glanced over to see an elderly man with all white hair, wrinkled, weathered-looking skin, and a slightly hunched-back walk in. "Enjoy your coffee," Riaha groaned, clearly uneasy about who had just walked in. Afterward, she turned and walked back to the counter.

"Was it me, or was that weird?" Luke asked.

"Nope, not you. That was definitely weird." Lisa replied.

Moments later, Luke and Lisa heard a loud voice from the counter, "Hurry up! I haven't got all day!"

Luke turned around in time to see the older man toss money onto the counter, grab his coffee, and start toward the door. When the old man saw Luke watching him, he barked, "What the hell are you looking at?"

Luke snapped back, "Somebody who was apparently never taught manners."

As the old man walked to the door, he snapped back, "Go to hell!"

"You're closer to that than me," Luke said with an evil grin.

"Wrong, I've already been there, and it ain't pretty!" The old man barked as he walked out the door.

Riaha returned to Luke and Lisa's table a few minutes later and said, "I'm sorry about that. He's always like that."

"Who was that?" Lisa asked.

"His name is Henry Cobb. He supposedly used to be the town mechanic. He worked on all the town's vehicles. He's one of the Smugglers Cove seven."

"What's that?" Lisa asked.

Riaha replied, "They are sort of like celebrities around here, I guess you could say. As the story goes, when World War II started, seven of them signed up together. Two of them never made it home."

"Wow, that's crazy," Luke said, "what happened to the rest of them?"

Riaha replied, "Most went on to become prominent figures in the town. One died a couple of years ago from a heart attack, though. I think there's only four left now. There's a statue in the park dedicated to them."

"That's a nice gesture," Lisa said.

"It used to be nice, anyway," Riaha said sadly.

"What do you mean? It's not now?" Luke asked.

"It has been vandalized a few times over the years, so it's seen better days," Riaha replied.

Lisa said, "That's terrible. I don't see why anyone would do such a thing like that. Was the person ever caught?"

"Nope, not that I've ever heard of," Riaha replied.

"That's sad," Luke replied.

"Yeah, it is. Well, you guys drink your coffee before it gets cold, and let me know if you need anything," Riaha said, smiling before she walked off.

"She's a sweetie," Lisa said.

"Yeah, she is," Luke replied.

"Hey, now, finish your coffee before you get in trouble," Lisa replied, smiling. Besides, we need to get back to the lighthouse. I want to check in with the project manager one more time before he leaves for the night."

"Sounds good," Luke replied.

The pair sat there for another ten minutes, drinking their coffees and eating their danishes. Afterward, they left Riaha a nice tip on the table and quietly walked out of the coffee shop.

Once they returned to the lighthouse and checked in with the project manager, they were pleased to hear that the workers had accomplished more today than expected. With any luck, they could start moving in within a few days.

After the workers left for the day, Luke and Lisa ordered a pizza, and after it came, they made the trek up to the top of the lighthouse, ate pizza, and watched the amazing sunset.

After watching the stunning sunset, the pair decided to dive into the journals and see what else they could discover. Little did they know that what they would soon discover would change everything.

5

March 1942

It was a cool and brisk day in March when there was a knock on the door of Christof's home. Anna opened the door to find a young man standing there. Before she could say anything, the young man smiled and said, "Telegram for Christof Wolf."

Anna replied, "I'll take it for him. He's up in the lighthouse."

"Very good, ma'am," the young man said as he pointed at a paper on his clipboard and said, "please sign on the next open line saying you received the telegram, and I'll be off."

Anna signed where the young man indicated and handed the clipboard back to him. When he took the clipboard, he handed Anna the telegram in a sealed envelope, tipped his hat to her, and left.

Anna closed the door, turned and walked over to the kitchen table, and sat the telegram down to continue working in the kitchen. No matter how much she tried to put it out of her mind, she could not help but wonder if this telegram was from the mysterious Hans, who had paid them a visit a few months ago. After stopping and staring at the telegram, willing it to open, Anna finally snatched up the telegram and started up the vast winding staircase to the top of the lighthouse. Christof was at the top, observing a convoy getting ready to depart for England, who was in desperate need of supplies having already been at war with Germany for some time now.

A few minutes after starting the climb, Anna reached the lantern room where Christof sat with a pair of binoculars, watching the convoy. "What brings you up here?" Christof asked.

"We just had a visitor," Anna replied with a worried tone.

Before he could ask who it was, Anna held out the envelope, and as soon as Christof saw it, he froze and stared at it for a moment. "Now I see why you came up here," he replied, taking the envelope from her.

"Please tell me it's not from ... him," Anna pleaded.

Christof opened the envelope and then pulled out the enclosed telegram. It only took a moment for him to glance at the telegram then he handed it to Anna, saying,

"Greetings from home."

"What are we to do?" Anna asked with fear in her voice.

Christof took a deep breath and said sadly, "For the sake of our families, we will do what we must."

Anna thought briefly before finally saying, "We could kill him."

"What are you talking about, woman?" Christof asked, shocked.

"I could prepare a special meal for when he comes ashore," Anna said, "add a little rat poison and it would be his last meal."

"No. You heard Hans. If something happens, Germany will just send another. If they ever get wise to what happened, I fear our families back home will pay dearly for it."

"You are right," Anna replied with a touch of sadness in her voice, "I did not think things through."

Christof stepped towards Anna and wrapped his arms around her, saying, "It will be ok. Everything will be all right. Come, let's go downstairs. We need to prepare for our guest."

"What is there to do?" Anna asked.

"I want us to go to town and get whatever supplies we need for the next few days. I want to stay out of sight as much as possible."

Anna thought momentarily and said, "I could use a few things."

"Make a list, and the three of us will go in a little while," Christof replied.

"Even Thomas?" Anna asked.

Christof replied, "Yes. Considering who is about to show up, I want the townspeople to remember that we are a family, just as they are."

Two NIGHTS LATER, Anna slipped something into Thomas' food to ensure he would sleep through the night. If everything went as they hoped, young Thomas would never know anything about their unwelcome visitor from Germany.

That night, Christof and Anna stayed up all night, watching for anything unusual in the surf. Finally, shortly after two o'clock in the morning, Christof decided to go down to the nearby beach and look around.

Christof grabbed his flashlight and started for the door, "Be careful," he heard Anna say as he opened the door.

Christof paused, turned around, and said with a smile, "I will."

Christof closed the door and walked the short distance across the property to a group of trees. Once he was in the trees, he could move down the coastline for two hundred yards to a small beach. Since this was the only open spot where a small boat could come ashore, Christof figured this was where their guest would come ashore.

For the most part, the beach was deserted, especially this time of night. The only thing that concerned him was, sometimes, young couples would pull off the nearby road and walk down to the beach from the road for make out sessions on the beach.

Fortunately, as Christof looked around from the cover of the nearby trees, he didn't see anyone on the beach. With any luck, he could get the person ashore and back to the lighthouse without anyone seeing a thing.

Christof had been in the tree line for about thirty minutes when he suddenly saw a black shape in the churning whitewater of the surf. Christof watched as the shape slowly came closer to shore. As the shape got closer, using what little moonlight there was, he determined that it was a small inflatable raft just large enough for one person.

Christof slowly eased to the edge of the tree line, making sure to keep an eye on the raft the entire time. Just when Christof thought the person in the raft was going to make it ashore without incident, disaster struck. A wave larger than the others struck the inflatable from behind, spinning the little raft and flipping it over, dumping the person and his contents into the surf.

Christof glanced around once again and, after not seeing anyone, darted out of the confines of the trees to the beach. In moments he was in the knee-deep surf, fighting his way to where the man was struggling in the surf. Coughing and choking on the cold seawater, the man was surprised when Christof grabbed him under the arms and helped him to the beach.

Unsure of who his savior was, the man said, "Thank you for helping me. My boat started taking on water offshore and—"

"There is no need for that. I am the lighthouse keeper," Christof replied as the two struggled out of the surf.

"I have to get my raft and supplies," the man said.

"We will," Christof said, taking huge gulps of air as they staggered onto the beach, breathing heavily.

It took them another ten minutes to find and gather the small raft, backpack of supplies, and another soft-sided waterproof bag. After finally finding everything and getting it to the tree line, the man said through chattering teeth, "Help me bury this bag and the box. All I need for my mission is the backpack."

Christof and the as-yet-unnamed man began furiously digging a hole to hide half of the items he came ashore with. "What are these things?" Christof whispered.

"It's my escape plan," the man whispered back. "I have what I need for my mission in my backpack."

"Where are you going?" Christof asked out of genuine curiosity.

"You do not need to know," the man snapped, "now dig faster."

Before they got any further, both men looked at each other, knowing they heard the same thing ... voices.

Both men stopped and suddenly froze in horror. Not fifty feet away on the beach, a young couple had apparently stopped at the nearby road and walked out onto the beach holding hands. Christof and the supposed spy could only watch, hoping the couple would leave soon.

Neither dared to move for fear of giving away the fact they were there. As they watched, the young man tried to kiss his companion. Christof could hear part of the young man's conversation with the girl, saying, "Come on ... I'm leaving soon to go into the army. Who knows when I'll be back?"

The young girl said something to the effect of, "Well, you will have to do your best to come back now, won't you."

The young man replied with something Christof couldn't make out, and the girl replied sternly, "No."

Suddenly, the conversation must have taken a turn as the girl drew back and slapped the young man she was with, across the face. As soon as this happened, the young man backhanded the girl, who yelled out in pain, grabbing her cheek. Moments later, she was sobbing uncontrollably and stomping away from him but much closer to where Christof and the spy were.

All Christof and the spy could do was watch and hold their breath, hoping the love birds would change direction and return the way they had come. They watched silently as the young man jogged to catch up to the girl, asking her to stay. When she kept walking, he grabbed her and spun her around to face him.

Immediately, she took another swing at him but missed. His

blood now boiling, the young man snapped, "You should not have done that!"

The man balled up his fist and knocked the young woman to the ground, where she rolled over and began to get up in a futile attempt to get away. The young man walked up beside her as she scampered to get away, kicking her in the side.

Christof moved to get up and intercede on the young woman's behalf, but as he attempted to get to his feet, the spy pulled him back down and growled, "Nein! We mustn't blow my cover!"

Christof glared at the man he had just helped come ashore but reluctantly stayed where he was. As Christof looked from the spy back onto the beach, what he saw next horrified him as much as any battle he had been in during the war. Before he realized what was going to happen, the young man pulled out a knife and stabbed the young girl in the chest twice.

The woman screamed and struggled against the young man for a moment, but after plunging the knife into her chest for a third time, her hands fell to her side, and she stopped moving.

Now panicked at what he had done, the young man jumped up and ran. As he took off running, Christof and the spy were horrified to see the young man run off the beach near where they hid the spy's raft and supplies.

As the young man ran in their direction, he suddenly veered off to one side where Christof and the spy knelt; however, he came close enough to see them and instantly realized what was happening. In one terrifying instant, Christof and the young man locked eyes on one another ... each recognizing the other and what they were doing on the beach.

In that instant, the spy pulled his own knife and chased the young man into the darkness. A few minutes later, the spy returned, stared at Christof, and said, "He was too far ahead. I couldn't catch him. We must bury the supplies and get out of here. Did you know him?"

"I've seen him in town a time or two. He's a local, I think." Christof snapped.

Christof froze for a moment, taking in everything that happened, and bolted out onto the beach to check on the young girl without saying a word to the spy. As soon as Christof knelt beside her, he knew there was no life left in her.

"You cannot help her!" the spy said, "We have to get out of here."

"We can't just leave her!" Christof snapped.

"We have no choice. It will blow my cover and get both of us arrested. Is that what you want?"

"No! Of course not!" Christof snapped, "But what should we do?"

"We keep going! That's what we do. The kid said he was leaving to go into the military soon. He saw us, and we saw him! He won't say anything because if he does, that will mean giving himself up too."

"But what if—"

"But nothing!" The spy interrupted, "Let's go!"

Both men returned to the raft and excess supplies and finished burying them before returning to the lighthouse.

They stopped outside the lighthouse, where Christof grabbed the spy by the shoulders and said, "We do not speak to what we just saw once we enter my home. My wife never needs to know. Is that understood?"

"Agreed," the spy replied, "the less that knows, the better for all involved."

They entered the lighthouse to find Anna sitting at the table in the small dining area. As soon as they entered, she looked up and said, "Both of you need to get out of those wet clothes before you catch a chill."

Fifteen minutes later, both men had changed and sat at the table and ate a bowl of warm soup Anna had fixed. "Do you like it here?" The German asked.

"Yes, very much," Christof replied angrily, "I don't want to do anything to jeopardize our being here."

"Then why did you help me?" The spy asked.

"I had no choice. A man showed up here a month ago saying if I didn't, our families back home in Germany would be sent to labor camps. He knew their names, so we know he was not bluffing."

The spy took a sip of the soup and swallowed, warming his

insides. "I am sorry for that, but you should know that the Gestapo know everything at home. If they say they would do it ... believe them."

Christof and the spy finished their soup, and then the spy asked, "Where can I sleep for the night?"

Christof showed the man to a guest room then everyone turned in for the night.

The following morning, Christof awoke and went to check on their overnight guest. When he got to the room, Christof found the door open, and the man was already gone. Moments later, Anna came in and asked, "Where is he?"

"Gone," Christof replied, "He must have left in the middle of the night. We still need to stay here for a few days. We don't need to be seen in town right now. I wouldn't want to give anyone the impression that we have ever seen him before."

Anna agreed and walked quietly to check on their young son, Thomas. After that, she went to start a pot of coffee. Anna returned with a slight smile and said, "Thomas slept through it all. He never knew anything."

"That's good," Christof replied, "the less he knows the better."

Christof gazed out of the kitchen window overlooking the nearby ocean. As he stared out over the choppy water, Anna wrapped her arms around him and asked, "What is it, my love?"

"I am thinking about last night ... who that man was, what he was going to do, and things like that. Why?"

"You seem ... off, not quite yourself this morning," Anna said with her usually warm smile. "Are you sure nothing else is bothering you?"

Christof forced a smile and replied, "Nothing that a good cup of coffee won't fix."

"I ... I can't believe what I just read," Luke said, shocked. According to the journal, Christof was there and at least recognized who killed the girl.

"We have to tell somebody," Lisa replied.

"And tell them what exactly? That my great-grandfather was there on the beach when the girl was killed. Yeah, that will go over real good I'm sure," Luke replied.

Lisa asked, "Does the journal give any indication as to who the spy was who came ashore that night or what happened to him?"

Luke read the journal a little more in silence, then said, "Not specifically, but it does say that a man was killed two days later in a neighboring community after being stopped by a local sheriff because he was acting suspiciously."

"Is that all it says?" Lisa asked.

After reading a little more, Luke replied, "Apparently, the man tried to run after the sheriff found documents sewn into his jacket. Nobody knew who he was or where he came from. What do you want to bet that was the spy?"

"Sure, sounds plausible," Lisa replied. "What about the killer? Does it say who it was?"

"Give me a minute, and let me see," Luke replied as he skimmed the following few pages. After quickly reviewing them, he looked disappointed and said, "No. It doesn't seem like he did, but Christof very well could have left us a clue."

"How?" Lisa asked.

"Remember when we went to Riaha's Coffee Shop, and the grumpy old man walked in?"

"Yes, I remember. Why?"

"Do you remember what she said about him?"

About that time, the proverbial lightbulb went off in Lisa's head. She smiled and said, "The Smugglers Cove seven!"

Luke smiled and replied, "That's what I'm thinking. The killer very well could have been one of the seven."

"We still have to find a way to narrow it down some," Lisa said.

"Narrow it down? How exactly do we do that?" Luke asked.

"Tomorrow let's go to the coffee shop and talk to Riaha. She said something about a statue in the park dedicated to them. If we're lucky, their names will be on there."

Luke yawned and replied, "Yeah, I guess we could go check it out."

Lisa put the laptop down and said, "Come on, let's go to bed."

"It won't do any good to go to bed now," Luke said, "I won't be able to sleep after finding out what I just read."

Lisa smiled coyly and replied, "Who said anything about going to sleep?"

6

Toby Mitchell pulled his car into the nearby lot and parked in the parking spot reserved for him. Truth be known, he always got a kick out of the "reserved for mayor" sign, knowing it was his and his parking spot alone. He walked into the old three-story building renovated in the early eighties. In its previous life, the building was a mercantile for the local fishermen of the area. Now, the beautifully restored building was home to the mayor's office, city council and most things dedicated to running the small community.

As Toby walked to the small coffee shop that provided the much-needed caffeine for the building employees, he found that Sheriff Baxter was already standing in line. When the sheriff saw Mitchell walk, he said, "Morning, Mr. Mayor."

"Morning, Eddie. What are you doing here this early in the morning?"

"Actually, I was coming to see you. We need to talk about something."

"Oh, really now? What's that?"

"Not here ... too many ears. Let's meet in your office in about ten minutes or so."

"That would be fine," Mayor Mitchell said, "let me get my coffee, and I'll meet you in my office shortly."

Sheriff Baxter replied, "That will be perfect. I need to make a stop first, anyway. See you in ten."

After the sheriff walked off, and while Mayor Mitchell was waiting in line for his coffee, he wondered what could be so pressing that Baxter needed to speak with him this early in the morning.

Once Mitchell got his coffee and fixed it the way he liked it, cream, no sugar, he took a careful sip of the hot liquid and said, "Ah, that's a good cup of mud!"

Satisfied that his coffee was made just the way he liked it, Mayor Mitchell carefully walked to his office and, a few minutes later, was seated behind the rather large desk.

He had been there for about five minutes when there was a knock on his door, "Enter," Mitchell said as he looked up to see who was coming into his office, although he already had a pretty good idea of who it was.

As expected, Sheriff Baxter walked in. He closed the door behind him and said, "I hope I didn't catch you at a bad time."

"No, not at all. Have a seat. What's on your mind?"

After sitting across from the mayor, Baxter said, "I'm not sure if you know or not, but I got a call from Ruth at the historical center the other day, and she had a couple of visitors she wanted me to know about."

"Oh, really now? Who was it?"

"Yeah, and as it turns out, they were the new owners of the light-house. You know, the young couple that's turning the property into a bed and breakfast?"

"I see," Mayor Mitchell said as he sat back in his office chair, "and what did they want?"

"Ruth says they were just looking around and antique shopping, that sort of thing."

Mitchell replied, "Why do I get the feeling there's more to this story?"

"Because there is," Sheriff Baxter replied. "Apparently, the couple saw an old photo of the lighthouse and started asking questions."

"What sort of questions?"

"Apparently, this photo was the picture taken of the surrounding area when Sarah Harper was murdered. The couple asked about a mark on the photo, and Ruth, being Ruth, told them that's where the body was found, then she started blabbing about the murder to them."

Mitchell sat back, smiled, and waved his hand dismissively, "I wouldn't worry about it too much. That was over eighty years ago. There's no reason to bring that dark piece of our town's history back into the light again."

"No, there's not, but here's the problem. Ruth said the husband and wife were talking as they started to leave and mentioned something about finding a set of journals during their renovations.

"Now you have my attention," Mitchell said, "what else did they say?"

"Ruth said she asked about seeing the journals but the husband said it was mostly unreadable. Anyway, Ruth started in on the whole Nazi spy rumor, and they seemed more interested in that than in Sarah Harper's murder. Anyway, I thought you should know."

Mitchell replied, "Thank you for bringing it to my attention. Don't say a word about this to anybody. With any luck, it will simply go away, just like always."

"I won't say a word, but we may be able to solve the only murder our town has ever had. Shouldn't we at least try to do our jobs?"

The mayor thought for a moment and said, "Yes, of course, but you know just as well as I do that young girl was murdered over eighty years ago. Even if there was something in the journals, the chances of bringing someone to justice are slim to none."

"True, but there is no statute of limitations on murder," Sheriff Baxter replied as he stood up to leave.

Mitchell thought for a moment and said, "How about this? Why don't you go to the lighthouse and ask about the diaries? Tell them it's the only murder this community has ever had, and it's still unsolved.

Ask them if it's okay to look at the journals to see if they have a clue. It won't hurt to ask."

"That was my thinking as well," Sheriff Baxter said.

As the sheriff turned to leave, Mayor Mitchell said, "Uh, Sheriff, like I said ... keep this quiet for now. We wouldn't want to get anyone's hopes up about solving it before we know what's in the journals."

"I understand," the sheriff replied as he turned and walked out.

"Close the door behind you on your way out," Mitchell replied.

"Yes, sir, Mr. Mayor," Baxter replied as he stepped out and closed the door behind him.

As soon as the door was closed, the mayor picked up the phone on his desk, dialed a number, then waited. It took a moment or two for the person on the other end of the call to pick up, but as soon as Mitchell heard the old man's voice, he said, "We need to talk ... and soon ... four o'clock at the usual place will be fine."

LATER THAT AFTERNOON, Mayor Mitchell stepped out of his office, told his secretary he was leaving early to run an errand, and then walked out to his car. He got in and drove the short distance to the community park.

After parking, he walked into the one-acre park, beautifully decorated with different flowers. This brought all kinds of birds and small wildlife into the park. Mayor Mitchell walked to the center of the park, where a decorative fountain was surrounded by water adorned with a large marble eagle with his head bowed in reverence.

Under the eagle's bowed head was a bronze plaque with the names of seven members of the community who signed up together to go fight in World War II. Beside two names were small stars indicating that two of the men were killed in action during the war.

Mitchell sat and admired the fountain for a few minutes until another much older gentleman joined him on the bench. "So, what did you need to talk to me about, son?"

"The murder of Sarah Harper," Mitchell replied.

Irritated, the man said, "Not this ... again. That whole mess should be in the past."

"It was until somebody brought it into the present. Now there's a problem." Mitchell said, concerned.

"What sort of problem?" The older man asked.

Pausing a moment to let a couple walk past, the mayor said, "The young couple that has bought the lighthouse and is remodeling it found some journals on the property."

"What do they say?" The old man asked.

"That part's ... unclear at the moment, but there could be something about the Harper murder in there. If there is, Sheriff Baxter will have no choice but to reopen the case. I wish you would tell me about that girl's murder. I can't help if I don't know what's going on," Mayor Mitchell pleaded.

"I cannot tell you. It's called plausible deniability. Besides, I promised I would take it to my grave."

"Take what to your grave?" Mitchell pleaded

The older man simply shook his head from side to side and said, "No, son, it's better for the community this way."

"Dad, when I took over from you as the mayor, I promised to discharge the duties of my position faithfully, and I gotta say right now, I think you're preventing me from doing that." After an uneasy silence, Mayor Mitchell said, "I'm just going to come out and ask the question. Did you kill Sarah Harper?"

The elder Mitchell looked at his son with shock and surprise and said, "Absolutely not!" Suddenly, his voice turned from anger to sadness, and he said, "But I know who did."

"What?" Mayor Mitchell replied, shocked, "Dad, you have to tell me!"

"I can't, son," the older man said sadly.

"Dad, you're not making any sense. Why can't you?"

"I've said too much as it is." The elder Mitchell said, "If I say more, you will have to act, and neither of us wants that. Now drop it."

"Drop it! Dad, you have to be joking! You can't just tell me something like this and then tell me to drop it!"

"Keep your voice down, Toby," the elder man said, "I've said all I can say about the subject."

Before Toby could say anything else, the elder Mitchell got up and said, "Call your mother. She misses you," with that, he turned and walked off.

Toby sat there another moment or two by himself, shook his head from side to side, and snapped, "Damn it!" Then got up and walked back to his car.

Pulling up at home twenty minutes later, Toby got out and walked up the sidewalk to his two-story New England-style home. Before he even got to the door, it opened, and his wife, Holly, of nearly twenty years, was standing there. As he stepped onto the porch, she saw the look on his face and said, "Oh, no ... I know that look. What's wrong?"

"Just family drama," Toby said as he walked in and poured himself two fingers of vodka.

After he poured himself a drink, he walked over to the couch, plopped down, and said, "He just doesn't get it."

"And just who are you talking about?" Holly asked.

"My dad, of course."

Holly rolled her eyes and said, "I should have known. Now, what is it?"

Toby forced a smile and said, "Nothing you need to worry your pretty little head about."

"When you say it like that, I'm not so sure I believe you," Holly replied as she bent down and gave Toby a peck on the lips, "just be careful."

"I will, my love," Toby replied, "I will."

7

The contractors were at the lighthouse bright and early, and after a short meeting with the project manager, Luke, and Lisa went to the apartment they still had for the rest of the month. Along the way, they stopped at several places and picked up free boxes to continue packing the rest of their belongings.

After spending several hours at their old apartment packing boxes and putting them into the box truck, they were ready to make the trip back to the lighthouse. As the time grew closer, Luke and Lisa smiled excitedly as they left their old apartment with a truckload of things to begin moving into the lighthouse once and for all.

On their way back to the lighthouse, during a lull in the conversation, Lisa's stomach let out a large growl. Lisa giggled and said, "I think my tummy is trying to tell me something."

Chuckling, Luke replied, "It sure sounds like it. You wanna stop at the little diner up the road for lunch?"

"Sounds great to me," Lisa replied. "Then we could unload all this stuff at the lighthouse, check in with the project manager, and make a coffee run."

"Now that sounds like a plan," Luke said with a smile.

After the unplanned stop, the two were back on the road and

pulled up at the lighthouse an hour later. As they hopped out of their car, Joe, the project manager was coming down the steps smiling from ear to ear, "Glad you guys are back," Joe said.

"That could either be good or bad," Luke said hesitantly.

Joe smiled and said, "Relax, it's good news. I have a surprise for you."

"What's that?" Lisa asked with a sigh of relief.

"All the renovations are complete. With just a few touch-ups, we will be ready for a last walk-through."

"Everything's complete?" Lisa asked excitedly.

Joe smiled and said, "Everything's done. You have a brand-new kitchen, bathrooms, and living areas. The picture window and bench came out perfectly so your guests can sit and read during the day and have a perfect place to watch the sun come up if they want."

"Let's go in!" Lisa said with excitement.

Joe smiled and said, "Lead the way. Just don't touch any of the walls. They could still be wet. You'll want to leave some windows open for a time to let the ocean breeze come in and air everything out to get the paint smell out. I figure one more day, and it will be all yours."

Luke and Lisa walked into their newly renovated lighthouse and looked around in total awe at what Joe and his contractor, Shawn, had done with the entire property.

As they went through each room, Joe and Shawn pointed out all the things that had been done along the way. All the rooms were painted a light and airy color, some tans but mostly blue-green tints to match the surrounding area and ocean.

Lastly, they walked into the kitchen, which boasted a large window over the sink that allowed a person to look out over the ocean while preparing food or cleaning up. Also in the kitchen were brand-new professional-grade black appliances with white cabinets. To finish off the kitchen, Luke and Lisa had selected a stunning example of Azurite Granite imported all the way from Brazil, which had stunning hues of blues, grey and a smattering of tans coursing throughout the countertops.

Lisa walked into the kitchen, and the sight took her breath. "This looks even better than I had imagined it would!" Lisa said as she walked in and looked around.

"And the grey flooring came out amazing!" Luke replied.

Joe and Shawn beamed with pride at seeing Luke and Lisa's reaction to the work they had done. Luke and Lisa said, "We can't thank you both enough for all the hard work you've done around here ... but to make it up to you once we're up and running, we want you to come to spend a few days with us free of charge, of course, to enjoy what you have worked so hard to build for us."

Joe and Shawn smiled and said, "You have a deal!"

After they chatted for a few more minutes, Luke and Lisa decided to go into town and have a cup of coffee at Riaha's. A little while later, the two pulled up and hopped out, eager to talk to Riaha.

As they walked in, the first thing they noticed was that Riaha was not behind the counter. Instead, it was another lady neither had seen in the past. As they walked up to the counter, the lady smiled warmly and said, "Hi and welcome to Riaha's. What can I get for you?"

Lisa said, "Wow, this is the first time we've been here, and Riaha wasn't here."

"The lady smiled and said warmly, "Even though it's her place she still needs to take time off too. My name is Josephine, and I will be glad to help you this afternoon."

"Sounds great!" Luke replied, smiling, "We will have two medium coffees with a splash of cream and two cheese danishes, please."

Josephine smiled and said, in a tone reminiscent of a children's Sunday School teacher, "I will bring your order right over. You two just have a seat anywhere you like, and I will have it shortly."

Luke and Lisa thanked Josephine then walked over and had a seat near the front of the coffee shop so they could look out into town. "Should we still ask?" Lisa asked.

"I don't see why not," Luke replied, "Josephine is bound to know where the memorial is for the Smugglers Cove seven."

A few moments later, Josephine came over, carefully set their order on the table, and asked, "Is there anything else I can get for either of you?"

"We're fine but we do have a question," Luke replied.

"And what would that be?"

Luke said, "The last time we were in here, Riaha told us about a small park nearby with a memorial to the Smugglers Cove seven. Do you know where it is?"

Josephine smiled brightly and said, "I sure do. It's easy to find and not far away. I will be glad to tell you how to get there."

"Fantastic," Lisa said.

"Tell you what, when you're finished, just come on over to the register to pay, and when you do, I'll tell you how to get there," Josephine said, smiling.

"What do you think we're going to find?" Lisa asked.

"Honestly ... I have no idea," Luke replied, "but maybe it will lead us to somebody."

"Yep, we won't know until we get there and have a look around," Lisa shot back.

The two finished their danishes and coffee and then went to the counter, where Josephine was waiting for them. After paying for their orders, Josephine gave them directions, which they found were spot on and they had no trouble finding the park after they left.

Once they parked, the pair got out and started to stroll through the beautifully landscaped yet small park. As they made their way to the middle of the park, they could see several walkways leading toward a decorative fountain with a large eagle on top with his head bowed down, and several benches around the fountain.

As they walked around to the front of the fountain, they stopped at a bronze plaque with the names of seven men on it. Lisa took out her phone and took a close-up picture of the plaque with the men's names on it for reference.

"So, now what do we do?" Lisa asked.

"Well, we can probably narrow the list down by two," Luke replied as he looked at the plaque, "I've seen lists like this before, and the stars usually represent men who were killed in action, so it's a good bet the bottom two men never made it home."

"That still leaves five names, and truthfully, we're not really sure the killer is on there," Lisa replied.

"No, we're not, but it's a starting point," Luke replied.

"So, the question still stands. What do we do now?" Lisa asked.

"We could go back and talk to the old lady at the historical center, but I'm not so sure I trust her after what happened with the sheriff," Luke replied.

"Yeah, I know what you mean. I guess the only real thing we can do is go back to the lighthouse and dive into the journals more. There almost has to be a clue in there somewhere," Lisa said.

"It's better than nothing," Luke said, "let's get out of here."

After a nearly twenty-minute ride back through town and out to the lighthouse, Luke and Lisa pulled up to see one of the town's three sheriff's cars sitting out front.

Luke and Lisa glanced at each other, and Lisa said, "This can't be good."

"Let's go see," Luke replied.

Luke slowly drove up the driveway to the lighthouse and parked. Before they even hopped out, Luke and Lisa saw Sheriff Baxter hopping out of his car and putting on his hat.

Luke and Lisa got out and Baxter approached them smiling, "Man, this place is beautiful compared to what it's looked like in years past."

"Thank you," Luke said. "Did you come all the way out here to see the renovations, or did you need something?"

"Actually, I came to see you two," Sheriff Baxter replied, smiling.

"Oh, and what about," Lisa asked.

Baxter pushed his hat back up and said, "Well, ya see, Ruth over at the historical center mentioned to me in passing that you had found a set of diaries or something on the property, and I was wondering if I might be able to take a look at them."

"I'm sorry, sheriff, but they are mostly unreadable," Luke replied. "We found them on an old, recessed bookshelf that had been plastered over for some reason, but the ones we've looked at were in terrible shape."

Lisa piped in, saying, "Yeah, we just pitched most of them and the others are so fragile we haven't opened them yet."

Baxter looked disappointed and said, "That's too bad. I was hoping that it may have had a clue into who killed Sarah Harper way back in 1942. It's our only unsolved murder ... as a matter of fact, it's the communities only murder that we know of, so it would mean a lot to folks around here if we could close it once and for all. I'm not trying to rush you because I see you have a lot going on here right now, but when you look at them, if you see anything at all in there about Sarah Harper, don't hesitate to call."

"We will call you if we find anything at all about her. Just so we'll know, what are you hoping is in there? Or what should we be looking for?"

"It was such a long time ago. Honestly, I don't know what to tell you to look for; just be on the lookout for the name Sarah Harper or anything else of relevance."

"We sure will," Luke replied as the sheriff handed Luke his business card.

Both Luke and Lisa watched as the sheriff got in his car, slowly turned around, and drove down the long driveway back to the main road. "Ok, was it me, or was that strange?" Lisa asked.

"That was definitely strange," Luke shot back, "which is why I was glad you didn't slip up and tell him anything about what kind of condition the journals are really in."

"Yeah, I wouldn't want the sheriff to 'confiscate' them, never to be seen again," Lisa replied.

"I know what you mean. I was thinking about the whole murder story on the way back to the lighthouse, and I'm not so sure somebody is telling us the truth. Is it me, or are people still incredibly hung up on a supposed murder that happened over eighty years ago?"

"No, it's not you. I was thinking the same thing," Lisa remarked.

After the workers leave, we need to go line by line through the journals. There has got to be something in there."

"That's exactly what I was thinking," Luke said excitedly.

After the sheriff left, Luke and Lisa checked in with Joe and Shawn, who told them that they would definitely be finished with the touch-ups tomorrow and would be able to turn everything over to them.

Once Joe and Shawn left for the day, Luke and Lisa sat on their new picture window bench with the journals and began to read. Before they knew it, they had drifted back to another time when World War II raged in Europe, but death was closer than ever...

CHRISTOF SAT WRITING in his journal at the table one morning; it had been three days since his visitor, and he had just come back from his first trip into town since that time. He had found out from his friend at the general store, Joseph, that a man in the next town over was killed by their sheriff after finding what turned out to be forged documents sewn into the liner of his jacket.

Joseph showed Christof a local newspaper with a headshot of the man who had been the suspected spy, and there could be no doubt that it was his visitor from the other night. Christof picked up a few much-needed items from Joseph at the store and went straight back to the lighthouse. He did not want to give anyone in town the chance to question him about anything for fear of slipping up.

On the drive back to the lighthouse, Christof was stopped by the local sheriff, Tom Baxter, who asked him if he had seen a young woman from town on the roads anywhere. Christof told the sheriff no, who then looked at him suspiciously for a moment or two, apparently picking up on Christof's nervousness. After looking at Christof warily for another moment and glancing around his truck, he proceeded to tell Christof to be on the lookout for a missing girl from town and then let him go about his business.

Christof drove straight home and told Anna what he had heard about the spy. However, he did not say anything about the missing girl from the town. He had yet to say anything to Anna about witnessing the girl's murder. If he had his way, he never would, knowing full and well that she would prod him into making a story up about why he was on the beach that night.

After unloading the supplies he had gotten in town, Christof went to the top of the lighthouse under the guise of checking on the lens and having a look at the shipping lanes. He was up there for about two hours, and he could see people searching the woods and the sides of the road for the missing girl, whom he already knew was dead. At the rate they're going, it would only be another hour or two before they found her body on the beach. After she was found, the next few hours would be very telling for Christof and his family.

8

Sheriff Tom Baxter had been up since four o'clock that morning talking to Sarah Harper's parents about where she could have gone or whom she could have been with the previous night. He had already talked to her parents, who told him that she had a date last night but never told them who she was going out with.

Truth be known, the sheriff and Sarah had already had a couple of run-ins. Sarah had a reputation for being a party girl and an 'able Grable' amongst the local teenage boys, but nothing to explain her sudden disappearance.

Sheriff Baxter had rounded up several people from the town and organized a search party, but two days later, he still had found no trace of her. With all the normal places checked inland, the search team moved down the coast and towards the lighthouse, using the lighthouse as a landmark.

Sheriff Baxter went to a slight rise near the coast and began surveying the area with his binoculars. As he looked around, the lighthouse came into view, and he could clearly see a figure on top of the lighthouse near the lenses. Although Baxter could not tell for sure, it appeared that the person at the top of the lighthouse was watching them. Whether the person was simply being nosy or had other nefarious reasons for watching, he wasn't sure ... but he was going to find out.

Before he could even think to start heading toward the lighthouse, his attention was drawn to a commotion on the nearby beach. Baxter went to the beach, where several people were guarding a particular area. Before he even got there, he could tell by the people's reactions that the news wasn't going to be good.

As he walked through the trees to the edge of the beach, one of the searchers walked up and told him that they had found her, and she was gone. Sheriff Baxter looked at the girl and immediately saw the stab wounds to her chest and knew it was no accident.

After recovering the body and notifying the parents, Sheriff Baxter began the arduous task of getting to the bottom of who killed Sarah Harper and why. He didn't know anything yet, but he had an idea of where to start.

Late in the afternoon, after consoling the family, Sheriff Baxter drove out to the lighthouse and knocked on the door. Christof opened the door and asked, "Yes, can I help you, sheriff?"

Sheriff Baxter stared at Christof for a moment, then said sternly, "I wanted to tell you that we found Sarah. Or did you already know?"

"No, I did not know," Christof replied nervously.

"Well, we just recovered her body by the beach not far from your lighthouse. You wouldn't have happened to see anyone around there a couple of nights ago, would you?" Baxter said as he watched Christof's reaction suspiciously.

"No, I did not," Christof replied as Anna walked up behind him.

Baxter made eye contact with Anna and asked, "What about you? Did you see anybody around the beach area a couple of nights ago?"

"No, I did not," Anna replied.

"Well, it's kind of funny that this lighthouse is the only place around, and neither of you saw anything," Baxter snapped, "What were you doing watching us earlier?"

Christof replied, "I was cleaning the lenses when I saw all the commotion on the beach and became curious."

"And that's all?" Baxter asked.

"Yes," Christof replied monotoned.

"Did you see any car lights or anything?"

"No," replied Christof, "we saw nothing. We were inside all night."

Baxter said, "Listen, Christof, I know you haven't been treated the nicest, but anything you could tell me would be a great help. I got the call at four o'clock in the morning two days ago and have been going almost nonstop since."

"I'm sorry, sheriff, but I don't know anything," Christof reiterated.

"Well, if you think of anything ... don't hesitate to let me know," Sheriff Baxter said. After that, Baxter turned and walked back to his car and drove away.

As soon as Christof closed the door and turned around, Anna asked, "Christof, what's going on? You know something. Don't you? I can see it on your face."

"It's best if you do not know," Christof replied.

"Christof, I'm your wife. Tell me what's happened," Anna pleaded, "Two nights ago was when our visitor came to be with us. Did you see something? Did the visitor do something?"

"No. And that is all you need to know. Now leave it alone, woman," Christof snapped before brushing past her, going into the bedroom, and closing the door.

Just then, Anna heard young Thomas walking up behind her and asked, "Mama, what's wrong?"

"Oh, nothing dear ... run along and find something to do," Anna replied.

Not long after the sheriff's visit, Christof came back out of their room with his journal and pencil in hand. He walked over to the table near the kitchen and took a seat. As he sat, Anna walked over, stood behind him, wrapped her arms around him, and gave him a reassuring hug.

"Are you ready to talk to me now?" Anna asked lovingly.

Christof took a deep breath and replied, "I have seen some terrible things in my life."

Anna sat down beside him and intertwined her arm with his and said, "What happened?"

Christof took another deep breath and said, "I went down to help our guest, and his rubber raft turned over in the surf. We spent the next twenty or thirty minutes finding all his things on the edge of the surf and took them to bury near the tree line. As we were burying the items, a young couple walked out onto the beach. They started fighting, and we watched as he stabbed her and killed her."

Anna said shocked, "That's terrible! Why didn't you do something to help?"

"I tried, but the visitor wouldn't allow me to because he was scared it would expose him."

Anna sat there briefly then asked, "Did the killer see you? Are you in danger?"

After a brief pause, Christof replied, "That is what I was about to tell you. After it happened, the killer ran, but he ran close enough to see me, the visitor, and what we were doing. There's no doubt that he knows who I am ... because I recognized him also."

"My God!" Anna snapped, "What's going to happen now?"

"Hopefully, nothing," Christof replied, "right before the argument happened, the boy said he was getting ready to go into the military. With any luck, he will be killed in the war, and nobody ever needs to know."

"What do you mean?" Anna asked.

"The visitor is already dead, so the only people who know what happened on that beach are the killer and me. He can't say anything to the sheriff about me helping a spy come ashore without giving himself away."

Anna paused a moment, then asked, "Do ... do you know who killed her?"

"I've seen him in town. I don't know his name, but he lives here for sure," Christof said.

"Are you telling me the truth, or do you just not want to tell me?" Anna asked.

Christof replied, "I would never lie to you, my wife. I have seen him before, but I do not know his name. Hopefully, I never will. Like I said, "With any luck, he will not come home from the military."

"Well, that sucks," Luke said disappointed.

"Now, what do we do?" Lisa asked.

"Truthfully, I'm not sure." Luke said, "But that most likely means the killer is one of the seven."

Lisa thought for a moment and said, "What we could do is ask around to see when the Smugglers Cove seven signed up and left and then see when Sarah Harper was murdered, and that could give us a good starting point."

"Who could we ask, though, without arousing any suspicion that we're asking around?" Luke asked.

Lisa smiled and said, "Well, I don't know about you, but I'm always up for a cup of coffee in the mornings."

"I like the way you think," Luke replied as he let out a long, drawn-out yawn.

Lisa said, "Let's get some sleep. With any luck, we'll be able to figure something out tomorrow."

Luke and Lisa awoke the next morning, ate a small breakfast, and waited for Joe, the project manager, and Shawn, his contractor. Joe and Shawn arrived at about eight o'clock that morning as usual and started the process of touching up some spots where needed.

Before Joe and Shawn got to work, Luke and Lisa told them they needed to run a few errands in town, and they would be back shortly. Afterward, the two went into town Riaha's Coffee Shop for a cup of coffee and, with luck, some information.

During the ride into town, Lisa asked, "Considering everything we've read and found out so far, what do you think happened?"

Luke thought about it for a moment and said, "I'm not sure exactly, but I was lying in bed last night thinking about something. What if the killer made it through the war?"

"What do you mean?" Lisa asked.

"What I mean is ... according to Christof's writing, he hoped the killer would not survive the war. What if he did, and that somehow led to Christof's demise?"

Lisa thought about it for a moment and said, "I see what you're saying, but Christof died in the fifties, close to a decade after the war. If it were the killer, wouldn't he take care of Christof as soon as he came back? Why wait for nearly a decade?"

"True," Luke replied as they pulled up to the coffee shop, which had become their new favorite place.

As Luke and Lisa walked into the shop, they were pleased to see Riaha behind the counter, "What's up, you two?" Riaha asked with her warm and friendly smile, "I haven't seen you in a while."

Lisa replied, "We came in not too long ago, but you weren't here. There was a young woman behind the counter named Josephine, I believe. She was very soft-spoken, like a Sunday school teacher."

"That's Miss Josephine, and she actually is a Sunday school teacher too," Riaha said with a smile, "Miss Josephine is the absolute best."

"She was a sweetie to us, that's for sure!" Luke replied.

"She's like that with everybody, too," Riaha replied. "Anyway, what can I get for you this morning?"

"Something strong," Luke replied, smiling.

"Strong tasting or more caffeine?" Riaha questioned.

Luke asked, "Do ya have something kinda in the middle?"

"I sure do. I have a smooth, medium roast coffee from the Copan Region of Honduras that I believe you'll love!" Riaha said excitedly.

"Sounds great," Luke replied.

"Make that two of them," Lisa piped in.

"That's not a problem. I got you," Riaha replied with her usual lovely smile. "Anything else?"

They both looked at the display case full of pastries for a moment, and Luke finally said, "I'll have the usual."

"I think I'll try a scone this morning," Lisa replied, "they look yummy."

"You guys know the drill; take a seat anywhere, and I'll be right over with your order," Riaha said.

They thanked Riaha and walked over to their usual spot, which happened to be one of the only open tables.

Not long after sitting down, Luke and Lisa noticed another older gentleman walk into the shop and up to the counter. Both watched as Riaha smiled at the man and shook his hand across the counter.

Neither Luke nor Lisa could make out what they were saying, but Riaha and the older gentleman had a several-minute-long conversation and glanced in their direction a time or two during their conversation.

As Riaha got their order together, the gentleman walked over to the table with her. As she put their orders down, Riaha said, "Guys, this is Harry Crawford. He is the retired mayor. Now, he sits on the town council. Mr. Crawford ... this is Luke and Lisa Wolf."

Luke and Lisa both stood and shook hands with Mr. Crawford, who smiled politely and said, "Riaha here tells me that you are now the owners of the lighthouse, and you're turning it into a bed and breakfast, is that correct?"

"Yes, sir, it is," Lisa said proudly.

"So, have you finished renovations?" Crawford asked.

"Actually, the contractors are putting the final touch-ups on it as we speak, and with luck, by this afternoon, everything will be complete," Luke replied.

"When do you hope to have your first guests?" Crawford asked.

"We still have some moving to do, but hopefully, within a month, we will be ready for guests," Lisa replied.

"Well, if there's anything I can do to help, please let me know," Crawford said with the ease of a practiced politician.

"We will," Luke replied as Crawford walked off and stopped at a nearby table to talk to other patrons.

"Can I get you anything else?" Riaha asked.

"A little information, maybe? Lisa inquired.

"Like what?"

"Is there anybody else, other than that Ruth person at the historical center, that we can talk to about the Sarah Harper murder? Somebody ... impartial," Luke asked.

"Hmmm... let me think about it a few minutes," Riaha said as she glanced around and lowered her voice. Maybe I can point you in the right direction." She winked and said, "When you come up, don't forget your receipt."

After Riaha walked off, Lisa replied, "I'll bet it's going to be on the receipt again."

"Probably so," Luke replied as he bit into his cheese Danish.

After they finished their coffee and pastries, they walked up to pay. After Luke paid, Riaha folded the receipt in half and handed it to Luke, who slid it into his pocket. "Don't forget to check your receipt," Riaha said with a wink and a smile.

"Oh, I will," Luke replied, "Have a good day!"

"You too, and good luck!" Riaha replied as they headed for the door.

Luke and Lisa walked outside to their 2023 Jeep Cherokee and hopped in. Luke reached in, took out the folded receipt, and said, "We have a name, but there's a slight problem."

"And what's that?" Lisa asked as she watched Luke check something on his phone.

"Her name's Tessa and she's a blogger and columnist at a small local newspaper in the next town over. I just checked the GPS, and it will take about thirty minutes to get there."

"That's no big deal; it's just a ride through the countryside," Lisa replied with a smile. It sounds like a quick day trip."

9

Thirty-five minutes later, after a nice scenic ride, Luke and Lisa pulled into the next community. Following their GPS, they pulled up at what was once a grand old house that now serves as the office of a local newspaper. Luke parked in the small yet ample parking lot across the street, and they made their way across to what used to be a massive and elegant Victorian-style three-story home.

As soon as they walked in, Luke and Lisa saw an older woman sitting behind a desk, "Can I help you?" She asked.

"Yes, we're from Smugglers Cove, and we were told to come here to talk to someone named Tessa."

"Regarding what?" The secretary asked.

"The Sarah Harper murder," Luke replied.

As soon as she heard this, the secretary turned and called out over her shoulder, "Tessa, somebody needs to speak with you."

"I'm busy," a voice called out from another room.

"It's about Sarah Harper," the secretary replied.

Suddenly, the disembodied voice snapped, "I'm on my way."

"That always gets her attention," the secretary said with a smile.

Moments later, a short, younger woman with a somewhat stocky build, long brown hair, and glasses walked around the corner and said, "I'm Tessa. What is this about Sarah Harper?"

Luke asked, "Is there somewhere where we can talk?"

"We can go in our conference room. It's small but quiet and a little more private," Tessa replied as she led them through the office.

As Luke and Lisa followed closely behind Tessa, Luke made eye contact with Lisa and pointed at the two tattoos on each of Tessa's arms as she walked through the office, her arms swaying from side to side.

After walking down a small hallway, Tessa showed them into a room with a conference-type table in the middle and chairs around it. "Have a seat," Tessa said.

As all three sat down, Tessa asked, "So, what's this all about?"

Luke replied, "The murder of Sarah Harper."

"I gathered that," Tessa shot back. "Do you have information for me or what's this about exactly?"

Luke replied, "Well, I'm Luke Wolf, and this is my wife, Lisa. We just recently purchased the lighthouse in Smugglers Cove and—"

Before Luke could finish his sentence, Tessa interrupted, saying, "Wait a minute, Wolf. As in Christof Wolf?"

"Exactly," Luke replied.

"Okay, now you have my attention," Tessa said as she leaned forward, resting her arms on the table in anticipation of what Luke was about to say.

"Well, Lisa and I recently took ownership of the lighthouse and are turning it into a bed and breakfast. During our remodeling, we found something that could possibly shine a light on the young woman's murder, and we were told to come see you about it."

Tessa replied, "Well, I don't know who told you to come see me, but you've come to the right place, that's for certain. Sarah Harper was stabbed to death in 1942 and found several days later on the beach very near your lighthouse. Of course, there was no DNA or anything back then. As far as I know, nobody even looked for any fingerprints. More than likely, her killer will never be known and is, most likely, already dead ... unless you have information that could change that." Tessa said.

Luke glanced at Lisa, who gave him a slight nod. Then Luke replied, "During the renovations, we found an old bookshelf that was walled over with books still on the shelf. As it turns out, the books were not books at all but journals."

Tessa's eyes widened and she said, "Holy shit! Did you find the journals? Are they readable? What did they say? I have so many questions that I'm about to pee myself!"

Luke smiled at Tessa's response and said, "We didn't even know there were any journals until our contractor happened to be fixing a wall and found the recessed bookshelf purely by accident. Wait a minute. How did you even know there were journals?"

"It's simple," Tessa replied. "I have been looking off and on for years into Sarah's murder. After doing much digging, I discovered from a relative who used to own the general store in town that Christof came in about once a month or so and bought a new journal, but none were ever found. I always hoped they would turn up and were not lost over time."

"So, what do you know about the murder?" Luke asked.

"Before I get into that, can I get either of you something to drink? Coffee, tea, or bottled water?"

"No, thanks," they both replied.

"Ok, well, I'm going to step out for just a minute and get a pen and notepad, and I will be right back. Don't go anywhere!" Tessa said excitedly.

After Tessa stepped out, Luke smiled and said, "I think we've come to the right place."

"So do I," Lisa replied with a smile.

Moments later, Tessa returned with a pen, a notepad, a bottle of Mountain Dew, and a small container of goldfish crackers. Luke smiled at the container of goldfish, and Tessa said smiling, "Shush, don't judge."

Luke giggled and said, "Whatever floats your boat. So, what do you know about the murder?"

"I know that in 1942, Sarah Harper supposedly had a reputation for being a wild child. Apparently, she had a new boyfriend every month or so. She supposedly started seeing a new young man a few days before she was murdered, but nobody knew who it was. She was secretive about it, which leads me to believe it was somebody from an affluent family in Smugglers Cove. What do the journals say? For the love of God, tell me Christof knew who it was. Or was it him? Did Christof do it?" Tessa said, firing off questions in rapid succession.

"Why would you ask that?" Lisa replied out of curiosity.

Tessa said, "There were many in the town that believed Christof was the killer or at the very least knew about the murder before the sheriff did because, from the top of the lighthouse, you could see most of the beach at that time. The tree line is grown up, so it's higher now, but back then, it was a straight view to the beach."

"So, why did they suspect Christof though?" Luke asked.

"As the story goes, the girl was missing for two or three days. During this time, the sheriff organized a search for her. Well, on the day her body was found, the sheriff stopped Christof in his truck as he was coming from town. Supposedly, Christof was nervous about something. Tom Baxter, the sheriff at the time, looked around his truck, but he didn't find anything, so he let Christof go."

"Baxter, Baxter, Baxter," Luke repeated, "why does that name sound familiar?"

"Probably because his son is the sheriff now," Tessa said.

Luke snapped his fingers and said, "That's it. We ran into him already."

"If you met him already, that means he wanted to introduce himself to you and let you know who was in charge. Anyway, later the same day, Christof was stopped. According to the reports, Sheriff Baxter and a group of townspeople were searching the shoreline near the lighthouse. The sheriff saw someone, presumably Christof, watching them from the top of the lighthouse. Not long afterward, they found Sarah's body on the beach."

"Yeah, but that's still a stretch to think Christof had something to do with the murder," Luke replied.

"Oh, I know, but there's more," Tessa said after she grabbed a handful of goldfish and sipped her Mountain Dew. The sheriff began to suspect Christof because he was so curious. Anyway, he went to the lighthouse that afternoon, and both he and his wife, Anna, were acting cagey as hell.

"Was there any proof ever found?" Lisa asked.

"No direct proof, but after Sarah's murder, the Wolfs began keeping to themselves, which only made the rumor mill worse. Strangely enough, it seemed to get worse after the war was over." Tessa said.

After hearing this, Luke and Lisa glanced at each other, and before either one could say something, Tessa snapped, "What was that look for? You two know something, don't you? If you know something, you have to tell me!" Tessa said excitedly.

Luke asked, "What do you know about the rumors of Christof helping a German spy come ashore?"

"Just that there were rumors, and that there was an unknown man killed by a sheriff in the next town over that had forged documents on him, but nobody ever found out who he was or where he came from. Why? The anticipation is killing me!" Tessa said with excitement as she grabbed a handful of goldfish.

Luke smiled and said, "Keep in mind that we haven't read all the journals yet, but Christof did, in fact, help a spy come ashore and—"

Tessa's eyes widened, and she slammed both hands down on the conference table with excitement and said, "NO WAY!"

"Oh, yes, and there's more," Luke said, grinning at Tessa's reaction. "It was the same night that Sarah Harper was murdered."

Tessa's eyes widened at the implications of what Luke just had said and the room was eerily quiet for a moment while Tessa worked it out in her head. "Did ... did the spy kill Sarah?"

"No, neither Christof nor the spy killed Sarah Harper. There was somebody else on the beach that night."

"Oh, holy shit!" Tessa snapped, "Who was it?" Tell me you know who it was!"

Luke said, "Unfortunately not ... but Christof was there when it happened."

Tessa, who had been writing everything down, stopped, looked up at Luke, and said, "He was there! What did he write?"

"Not much, I'm afraid. Christof wrote in the journal that he saw the murder, but the spy wouldn't allow him to help the girl for fear of giving him away, but then it all went haywire after the murder. The killer ran right past them. Christof wrote in the journal that he recognized the kid as a local but didn't know his name. He also wrote that he heard them talking, and the killer supposedly said he was about to go fight in the war. Christof then wrote that he hoped he got killed overseas."

Lisa joined the conversation, saying, "With that said, we were wondering if you could help us narrow something down. Have you ever heard of the Smugglers Cove seven?"

"Actually, I have. Why? Do you think the killer could be one of the seven?"

"We don't know, but if the murder happened just prior to the seven leaving for boot camp ... it is possible, and if the rumor mill got worse after the war, which could mean—"

"The killer made it home!" Tessa blurted out, interrupting Luke mid-sentence. "That means the killer at least knew who Christof was and knew he ran the lighthouse."

"How many of the seven are still alive?" Lisa asked.

Without hesitating, Tessa replied, "Four, two died in combat, and one died a few years ago of a heart attack."

"So, there's a chance that one of the four is a killer," Luke said.

"What can I do?" Tessa asked.

"What can you tell us about the four that are left? Lisa asked.

"Well, Harry Crawford is the retired mayor. These days, he has a seat on the town council. Then there's Frankie Mitchell, who also sits on the council. His son, by the way, is the current mayor. Roy Parker is a retired doctor. He started as a medic in the army. He mostly keeps to himself, and the most colorful out of the bunch is a man named

Henry Cobb. Henry was the town mechanic. There wasn't anything he couldn't fix, so he worked on all of their vehicles until he retired."

"We ran into him at a coffee shop in town not too long ago," Luke said, "colorful is an understatement. Mean as a snake is more like it."

"So, I've heard," Tessa replied.

Lisa asked, "If you had to guess, who would be at the top of the list?"

Tessa sat back in her chair momentarily, taking in everything she just heard and said, "There's another component to this group that you don't know about."

"What's that?" Luke asked.

"The letters," Tessa replied.

"What letters?"

Tessa said, "A man named Robert Delaney was one of the seven, but he was the one who died of a heart attack several years ago. At his funeral, his widow was given an old and worn letter by the retired sheriff, Tom Baxter."

"What was the letter?" Lisa asked.

"I don't know exactly, but I did find out later that each member of the seven wrote a letter to family or whomever, saying whatever they wanted to get off their chests in case they didn't make it home. Since the sheriff was exempt from service, he was chosen as the keeper of the letters."

"Why didn't he return the letters when the survivors came home?" Luke asked.

"Apparently, there was a pact that the letters would only go to the next of kin after the person died, no matter whenever that was. Rumor has it that Harry Crawford tried to get his letter back for years, but the sheriff wouldn't budge."

"What happened?" Luke asked.

"Rumor has it that's why Crawford ran for and won the mayoral election. When he won the election, the theory is that he tried to force Sheriff Baxter to give him the letter back, or he would fire Baxter."

Lisa said, "There must be something in that letter that Crawford does not want to get out. You don't suppose Crawford is the killer, and he confessed in the letter, do you?"

"The thought had crossed my mind," Tessa said, "but it's highly doubtful. The Crawfords and the Harpers were from different socioeconomic groups. The Crawfords were well off, and the Harper family were fishermen. They would have never crossed paths."

"How do you know all of this?" Luke asked.

Tessa smiled deviously and said, "Let's just say ... I have an inside source."

"Oh, really now. Anybody we might know?" Lisa asked, not really expecting Tessa to say.

"Have you been to the historical center in Smugglers Cove yet?" Tessa asked.

"Yeah, we went a couple of days ago and looked around. There was some old woman in there named Ruth, I think. She was fine until she realized our last names. Then she got real weird," Luke replied, "Wait, is that your source?"

"Yep, the one and only. That's dear old mom," Tessa confessed.

Luke's eyes widened, and before he could catch himself, he asked, "Ruth, is your mother? Oh wow! I didn't see that one coming. Wait a minute! That means you must be Baby Ruth!"

"I know, right?" Tessa shot back, her cheeks turning red with embarrassment. "Shocker, anyway; the two called an uneasy truce as they realized they were in a position that could be mutually beneficial to both parties and the town, for that matter."

"What happened?" Lisa asked.

"Apparently, over time, Crawford became less interested in the letter until it came time for Baxter to retire as sheriff."

"Then the cycle began again," Luke surmised.

"Exactly." Tessa replied, "Miraculously when it was time for the elder Baxter to retire, his son got the job."

"Nothing shady there," Lisa quipped.

"Nothing at all," Tessa shot back sarcastically, "but here's where it gets interesting. Nobody seems to know if Eddie Baxter knows about dear old dad's 'arrangement' of him taking over for his dad or not. For all he knows, he got the job on his own merits."

"What's with the boys club?" Lisa asked.

"Harry Crawford, Tom Baxter, and Frankie Mitchell all grew up together and were like brothers before the war broke out. They're kinda like the 'Old Guard,' if you will. Now, their kids have been groomed to take over for them."

Luke asked, "So if the killer is one of the four survivors, who is the most likely?"

Tessa thought momentarily and replied, "You won't believe who I think it is, and it's not who you may be thinking."

"Who?" Lisa asked with excitement.

"Before I answer, I want you to know that I have absolutely no proof of what I'm about to tell you. With that said, Roy Parker is at the top of my list."

"The retired doctor!" Lisa snapped.

"Yep. His parents were well off, like Sarah's parents. Roy Parker's father was a doctor, and he wanted to follow in his dad's footsteps. He ran in the same circles, so to speak. Parker would have known where to stab someone, ensuring he would hit vital organs also."

Luke and Lisa exchanged glances at one another, and then Luke replied, "It does make sense."

Lisa shot back and said, "But if it's the doctor, why was Harry Crawford so set on getting his letter back?"

"That's the big mystery," Tessa replied.

"Well, I think we have more reading to do," Lisa replied.

Before Luke could say anything, Tessa said, "Well, if there are any more questions or if you need any help in your research. I will help you wherever I can. I've been trying to solve this case for years, and now you have the journals; maybe you can."

As Luke and Lisa stood to leave, Tessa handed them a business card and said, "Call me anytime, day or night, if you find something."

"We will," Luke replied as they left the conference room and headed for the front door.

Once they were back in their car and pulling out for the drive home, Lisa asked, "So, what do you think?"

Luke replied, "I think we need to see if Joe and Shawn have finished. Then I think we have a lot more reading to do. That's what I think."

10

Once Luke and Lisa returned to the lighthouse, they were pleased to find out that all of the touch-ups were complete, and Joe and Shawn were ready to do a final walkthrough. After spending the next hour going through every room, Luke and Lisa were ecstatic with how everything came together and couldn't be more pleased with the workmanship of the project manager, Joe, and his contractor, Shawn.

After receiving the final totals and paying their outstanding debt to Joe, Luke and Lisa spent the rest of the day moving what was left of their belongings from their old apartment to the lighthouse.

By the time the sun had gone down that afternoon, Luke and Lisa had all their belongings at the lighthouse. Some of the items were still in the box truck sitting outside, but at least everything was here in one place, and they no longer had to return to their old apartment again.

After they took long hot showers, Luke and Lisa ate supper, which consisted of sub sandwiches they had picked up along the way back to the lighthouse. After eating, both took copious amounts of ibuprofen for their sore muscles and crawled into bed with the journals, hoping against hope that they would find something useful in them.

According to the journals, Christof and Anna kept to themselves after Sarah Harper's murder, only going into town when supplies or parts for the lighthouse were needed. Joseph, Christof's friend at the general store, filled him in on the latest gossip on Sarah Harper's murder and how the investigation was going.

Christof made it a point to be at Joseph's shop as soon as it opened so he could get in, get what he needed, and get out before much of the town was even awake. The last thing he needed was to mix it up with some local punks who think he had something to do with the murder.

On one such morning nearly two weeks after Sarah Harper's murder, Christof came into the store for supplies and to catch up with Joseph, whom he considered to be his only friend. "Good morning, Christof," Joseph said with a smile.

"Good morning, my friend," Christof replied, "Hope all is well with you?"

"Yes, everything is fine," Joseph replied warmly, "I have your order all ready for you."

"Fine, fine," Christof replied as Joseph entered the back room to grab Christof's order.

"I have a fresh pot of coffee on. Would you like a cup?" Joseph asked.

"Are you sure?"

"Why wouldn't I be?" Joseph asked.

"I've heard the rumors that people think I had something to do with Sarah Harper's murder, and I wouldn't want to put you in a bad position," Christof replied with a tinge of sadness in his voice.

"For one thing, this is my store, and I have coffee with whoever I want in my store. Besides, I know who buys what in the town, so nobody wants me to start talking. I assure you," Joseph said with an evil little smirk.

Christof could only chuckle as Joseph produced two cups of hot coffee, handing one to Christof. "How do you know I like my coffee black?" Christof asked.

"Easy. You order more coffee than sugar and milk, which tells me your wife is the only one in the family who uses them. I'd venture to say you drink two to three cups a day, more, of course, in the winter."

Christof looked at Joseph, smiled, and said, "Scheisse."

"What was that?" Joseph asked.

"Oh, sorry, sometimes, my German still slips out. I just said shit," Christof said with a smile, "Is there anything new with the murder case?"

Joseph took a deep breath and said, "Not a thing. Sheriff Baxter has no idea who did it or why. There's no murder weapon, no clues, no suspect ... nothing."

"Her family didn't know anything?" Christof asked.

"Baxter talked to them, and from what I've heard, they have no idea who she was out with that night or why she was near the lighthouse. It seems like the killer simply vanished," Joseph said.

"Somebody has to know who she was with. Don't they?"

"I would think so, but I did hear something the other day that the sheriff is looking into, although I don't think it's what happened," Joseph said.

"What is it?" Christof asked.

Joseph took a sip of his coffee and said, "Baxter was in here the other day, and he came up with a theory. Since he can't put anybody on that beach with her from town ... remember that mystery man I told you about who got shot and killed by the sheriff the next town over?"

"Yes, I remember," Christof replied.

"Baxter thinks that maybe he really was a spy, and somehow those two crossed paths, maybe as he was coming ashore and she saw him, so he had to kill her."

Christof thought for a moment, making sure to be extremely

careful with what he was about to say, and then he replied, "I'm not so sure of that, my friend. A German spy would have known to avoid her at all costs. He wouldn't allow himself to be discovered by a teenage girl as soon as he hit the beach."

"See! That's exactly what I told Baxter, too!" Joseph agreed. "I do want to tell you, though, that there are a few people in town who think you may have had something to do with the murder."

"I figured as much, but believe me, I have seen enough bloodshed," Christof said as he smiled and held up what was left of his arm, "much of it my own."

Joseph hesitated a moment and then asked, "Do you mind if I ask how it happened?"

Christof replied, "My regiment was dug in near a tree line, and the Americans didn't know we were there. They tried a straight attack first, which didn't work. Then, the artillery came. Shells were dropping all in our position, and one must have landed near me. The next thing I knew, it was a week later, and I was in a hospital in the rear."

"War is such a terrible, terrible thing," Joseph replied sadly.

"Were you there?" Christof asked.

"I was. I was in the Argonne Forest, so I understand. I still have nightmares."

"So do I," Christof replied. That's why I write in my journals. It helps." Christof finished his coffee and said, "Well, I hate to leave because I love our chats, but I need to get back. Can you just put this on my tab?"

Joseph hesitated momentarily, then said, "I will ... but you need to make a payment soon, my friend. I have bills to pay as well."

"I know, and I will pay soon. I promise," Christof replied, "You have my word."

"Your word is always good here, my friend," Joseph said with a friendly smile.

After the two shook hands, Christof picked up his supplies, turned, and walked out.

On the way home, Christof thought about what had happened that night on the beach, and suddenly, a thought came to him. What did he help the spy bury on the beach? All the way back to the light-house Christof wracked his brain, trying to come up with what it was that the spy could have been carrying that he wouldn't need on the main part of his mission.

Although times were vastly different from his time in service, he remembered hearing stories about how spies going behind enemy lines were given money to bribe locals. It had occurred to him that the now-dead spy would need money if he had any hope of escaping the United States.

Once he got home, young Thomas came out to the truck to help Christof bring in the supplies. As Thomas ran out, he said excitedly, "Guess what, father?"

"What, my son?" Christof asked.

"While you were gone, I saw another freighter leaving this morning traveling down the coast. It was sitting low in the water, so it was pretty full."

"That's great! Was it showing colors?" Christof asked.

"It sure was! It was flying a Columbian flag, so I bet it was heading back home!" Thomas replied excitedly.

The two walked inside with the supplies, and as soon as Thomas put what he was holding in the kitchen, he snapped, "I am going to my room right now and put it in my log!"

Anna watched him run off with a smile and said, "He couldn't wait for you to get home so he could tell you. He was so excited."

"I think that's great that he loves looking for ships as he does," Christof replied as he helped put the supplies away and set about the day of making minor repairs around the lighthouse.

That evening, after Thomas got up from the dinner table, Christof and Anna sat finishing their dinner. Anna asked, "Are you all right? You haven't said much tonight?"

"Yes, I'm fine. I've just been thinking about something off and on all day. That's all."

"What is it?" Anna asked.

Thomas spent the next twenty minutes telling Anna about what he knew about spies when he was in the army and the possibility that the spy could have had a significant amount of money on him when he came ashore.

After talking it over, it was decided that after Thomas went to sleep, Christof would go down to the beach and dig up what he and the spy had buried to see what he was carrying.

In the middle of the night, Christof kissed Anna, grabbed a flashlight and a shovel, and cautiously made his way down to the nearby beach. After sitting in the nearby tree line for another fifteen minutes, ensuring nobody else was on the beach, Christof went to the approximate spot where he and the spy were that night and started digging.

It took digging several small holes around the general location before he hit an object eight inches under the soft beach sand that he knew shouldn't be there. It took another few minutes of furious digging to open the hole enough for Christof to pull out a rubberized satchel especially designed to keep the contents from getting wet.

Quickly filling the hole back in as best he could, Christof grabbed the satchel and bolted into the relative safety of the tree line for a few moments. He sat there looking around, making sure nobody else was around. Once he felt it was safe enough, Christof left the trees and took a longer winding route back to the lighthouse to be on the safe side.

Anna saw Christof coming through the window, opened the door right before he got there, and quietly closed it as soon as he entered. "Well?" Anna asked, "What's in it?"

"We're about to find out," Christof replied as he made his way over to their dinner table. Anna looked on with curious excitement while Christof opened the satchel and started pulling out multiple items, from a complete change of clothes to forged documents, an American .38 handgun with a box of ammunition, and in the very bottom of the satchel was yet another sealed bag.

Christof took out the smaller sealed bag and cautiously opened the bag in the light. What he pulled out was astonishing. Christof and Anna's eyes widened with delight as they gazed upon a stack of money nearly six inches tall. "Mein Gott," Christof said shocked.

"How ... how much is there?" Anna asked, equally shocked.

Christof quickly looked through the stack of bills and found an assortment of different denominations. "I would say more than we would ever need in our lifetime," Christof said with a smile.

"What do we do with it all?" Anna asked.

Pausing a moment before answering, Christof replied, "We keep it. That's what we do with it. Nobody knows about this money except you and me because the spy is dead."

Anna thought momentarily and asked, "What about the killer, though? Won't he know something?"

"He doesn't know anything about what was in the satchel. All he saw was me and someone burying something on the beach. Chances are, he's already gone into the military by now anyway. I hate to say it, but if we're lucky, he won't make it back home."

"And if he does?" Anna asked.

"We will worry about that if it happens," Christof replied.

"So, now what do we do?" Anna asked.

Christof replied, "We'll keep the money, of course, but everything else has to go. I will take the rest and bury it somewhere it will never be found. After that, we need to find somewhere very safe for the money."

Since it was the middle of the night and nobody would be around, Christof took the spy's satchel, minus the stack of money, and once again left into the darkness. He arrived back at the lighthouse an hour later and said, "It has been taken care of. That satchel will never again see the light of day."

"And what about the other?" Anna asked.

"We will keep a very small portion of the money here for emergencies, and I need to go to the store and pay my tab with Joseph. After that, little by little, I will probably put it in the bank where it will be safe."

"Why not simply keep it here?" Anna asked.

"I wouldn't want people to wonder where the money was coming from," Christof replied, "anyway, nothing has to be decided right now. Let's go to bed. Tomorrow will take care of itself."

Bright and early the following morning, Christof took some of the money and went into town. As was the norm since Sarah Harper's murder, Christof was one of the first into Joseph's store when it opened. "Good morning, Christof," Joseph said as he opened the door and let Christof inside.

"Good morning, my friend," Christof replied, "How much is my tab?"

"Just a moment, and I will check for you," Joseph said as he walked behind the counter. Christof watched as Joseph opened the ledger he kept, found Christof's name, and began adding up his total. "I am sorry to say that it is seven dollars and fifty cents," my friend," Joseph said, "You need not pay it all. I was simply reminding you that I had not gotten a payment from you in a while."

"I know my friend, not to worry. I've come to pay what I owe you," Christof said with a smile as he took the money out of his pocket and paid Joseph.

Joseph smiled and said, "It would seem as if you have had some good luck come your way, my friend."

"You could say that," Christof replied, "I have just received quite a bit of back pay that I was owed, and now I have come to repay your kindness."

"Anytime," Joseph said with a smile, "I have it marked in my book, and you are paid in full."

"I can't thank you enough, Joseph," Christof said with a smile.

"Glad I could help," Joseph replied warmly.

As Joseph finished marking Christof's tab as paid, the bell on the store's front door rang, and both men looked up to see Sheriff Baxter walking in.

For a split second, Christof got extremely tense, but then, as quickly as it appeared, it went away as the sheriff smiled and said, "Hello, gentlemen. How are you this morning?"

Before Christof could respond, Joseph said, "Fine, just fine! Christof here has just come in to pay his tab, all seven dollars and fifty cents worth."

"Wow, that's one hell of a bill," Baxter interjected as he eyed

Christof, secretly wondering where the money came from. "It's always good for a man to pay his debts, don't you think?"

Christof forced a smile and replied, "Yes, of course. Well, I must be off. I simply came to town this morning to pay my tab. I will see you soon!" Christof said as he turned and headed for the door.

"Goodbye," Sheriff Baxter said.

"See you soon, my friend," Joseph replied warmly.

Christof walked out of the store without looking back; however, as he walked to where his truck was parked nearby, he glanced over his shoulder to see Joseph and the sheriff deep in conversation. Even though Christof trusted Joseph and considered him to be a friend, he couldn't help but think they were talking about him.

11

After reading for a while, Luke said, "Well, I guess that solves one part of the mystery."

"What do you mean?" Lisa asked.

"I don't have any way to prove it, of course, but I would venture to guess that what we just read explains where the mysterious trust money came from," Luke replied, "which means, if that's what happened we renovated this lighthouse with nazi money."

"True, but we can't know for certain, and even if it was, we're using the money for good, not evil as it was originally intended," Lisa said.

Luke was quiet for a moment, then replied, "I can live with that."

"So can I. Now, let's get some sleep, and hopefully, we will be able to find something else in the journal that will help narrow it down for us."

Luke and Lisa exchanged a brief kiss before settling down for the night. Luke carefully placed the journal he was reading on the night-stand while Lisa put her computer to sleep and turned off the light. Soon after, both fell into a deep sleep.

The next morning, Lisa awoke, yawned, and reached over to grab

Luke's hand but found the bed empty. Slowly as she awoke from her slumber, Lisa became more coherent and realized that not only was Luke not in the bed, he was nowhere in their room either.

Lisa got up, wrapped her robe around her, and stumbled down the hallway to the living room, where the morning sun beamed directly into multiple windows facing the ocean. As she entered the living room, the aroma of freshly brewed coffee waffled through the air.

"Coffee smells good," Lisa said, still half asleep.

"What are you doing up so early?" Luke asked.

"I just woke up and realized you weren't there," Lisa replied as she fixed her coffee and sat down beside him. "Whatcha reading?"

Luke took a sip of his steaming coffee and replied, "Oh, just more of the wartime journal. There's stuff in here about destroyers and bigger ships moving up and down the coast and such, but not much else about the murder or who may have done it. I did find one reference to Christof seeing someone hanging around the lighthouse but couldn't make out who it was."

"Was somebody watching the lighthouse or something?" Lisa asked.

"Christof doesn't say, but I'd venture to guess that it was probably Sheriff Baxter. The sheriff probably thought Christof did it but had no proof. He was probably hoping to catch Christof doing something suspicious and catch him in the act of getting rid of evidence or something."

Lisa took a sip of coffee and said, "I guess it's possible ... unless there's another explanation."

"Like what?" Luke asked.

Lisa thought for a moment and said, "What if it was the shop owner ... Joseph?"

Luke looked at Lisa and said, "You better take another sip of coffee or two. I don't think you're awake yet."

"No, I'm serious," Lisa said.

"Yeah, I know you are," Luke replied, "look, from everything we've read, Christof and Joseph were friends. Joseph was probably the only friend Christof had. What makes you think that Joseph was the one who could have been watching the lighthouse?"

Lisa grabbed her phone and did a quick Google search before answering, "Last night, you said Christof paid his entire bill of seven dollars and fifty cents all at once. In today's money, which would have been nearly one hundred and fifty dollars."

Taking another sip of his coffee, Luke replied, "Yeah, but that's a stretch."

"True, I was just pointing it out, that's all," Lisa said.

"I know, but my money is on Harry Crawford," Luke replied.

"Why?"

"Why else would he be trying to get that letter back so much unless he confessed to killing Sarah Harper?"

"It could be a lot of things," Lisa shot back, "He could have cheated about his age when he signed up for the army, or he knew something about somebody else in the town. There's no telling what could be in that letter."

"Yeah, but back then, he would have only been eighteen, maybe twenty years old, so chances are that he hadn't been around long enough to see or do anything."

"Yeah, you do have a point," Luke replied.

"So, what's on tap for today?" Lisa asked.

"We could go back to the historical society and talk to Ruth again. Maybe there is something else she can tell us."

"Are you sure that's wise, considering what she did last time we were in there?" Lisa asked.

"Not exactly, but she knows the circumstances and most of the people involved. Maybe she can put us in contact with someone from the Harper family."

"That's a thought," Lisa replied, but are we sure we want to mess with her again? We already figured out she's probably the gossip queen of the town. Or we could go back to the coffee shop and talk to Riaha. Something tells me she knows more than she's letting on."

"Now, that sounds like a great idea. I could use a cheese Danish,"

Luke said with a smile. "We need to take the car also because we have to take the box truck back today since we're done with it."

Lisa giggled, patted Luke's stomach, and said, "You keep eating those danishes, and you're going to need bigger clothes, mister."

Thirty minutes later, after getting ready, the pair drove into town and walked into Riaha's Coffee Shop. "What's up, you two?" Riaha said as she saw them walking in.

"Oh, the usual," Luke replied with a smile.

"I got you," Riaha said with her usual warm and friendly smile.

Luke and Lisa grabbed some napkins and took a seat near the front of the shop. Within a few minutes, Riaha walked over with their orders and asked, "Is there anything else?"

"Actually, there is," Luke replied. Is there anyone from the Harper family who still lives around here?"

Riaha thought about it for a moment, glancing around, and after not seeing anybody nearby, said, "Yeah, actually, there is. I don't know what her last name is now, but her first name is Brooke. She won't talk to anybody, though, about what happened to Sarah Harper. Since she's one of the last living relatives of Sarah Harper, she's been hounded over the years by different people and news groups about what happened, and I think she's just done with it."

"Well, we have some insight into the case that others don't," Luke replied, "would you be willing to reach out to her on our behalf?" We would love to talk to her."

"Sure, I can go after I close the shop today. Why don't you guys come back at the same time tomorrow, and I will hopefully have an answer for you?"

"Sounds like a plan," Lisa replied.

Before Riaha left the table, she saw someone walking down the sidewalk and said, "Here comes trouble."

Just then, the door chimed as someone walked in. Purely on instinct, Luke and Lisa both glanced up to see Henry Cobb, the gruff old man and one of the Smugglers Cove seven, walk into the shop.

They watched as the older man walked straight up to the counter and snapped, "Give me a black coffee!"

"Coming right up, Mr. Cobb," Riaha said.

Luke watched as Riaha handed him a cup of coffee. He tossed a few dollars on the counter, turned, and headed for the door. Before Lisa even realized what he was going to do, Luke hopped up and said, "Mr. Cobb, I understand you are one of the Smugglers Cove seven. Is that true?"

"Yeah, so what if I am?" the old man snapped.

"I'm Luke, and my wife and I just purchased and renovated the lighthouse."

"Yeah, so," Cobb barked.

"We found something pertaining to Sarah Harper's murder that might interest you. Did you know her?"

For a fleeting moment, Luke saw pain register in Cobb's eyes at the mention of her name. Cobb stiffened and said, "She's dead and buried. She was dead forty years before you were an itch in your daddy's pants! What could you possibly have that would interest me?"

As Cobb started to push past Luke and walk towards the door, Luke replied, "Christof Wolf was my ancestor, and I found his journals."

Cobb stopped dead in his tracks, turned, and said, in a somewhat softer tone, "You ... you have what?"

"It's a long story, but we found a set of journals that Christof Wolf wrote during and after the war, apparently until his death."

Cobb paused a moment, then snapped, "There's nothing you can do about anything. So, what if you have some Germans old journals?" Afterward, he continued toward the door.

As he opened the door, Luke called out, "We can figure out who killed her."

Cobb pushed the door open, turned around, and said, "Nobody can do that; they've been trying since the war, and nobody is closer now than they were back then." Before Luke could respond, Cobb walked out and disappeared down the sidewalk.

"That went well," Luke replied as he rolled his eyes.

"Yeah, but did you see his response when you told him about the journal and Sarah Harper? He knew her for sure." Lisa replied.

"Oh, yeah. He did," Luke replied as he took a sip of coffee.

Lisa stroked her chin as if she was thinking about something, and then she said, "Looks like we have some more investigating to do. Why don't we go back and have a chat with Tessa? Maybe she can shed some light on old Cobb there."

"Sounds good. What do we have to lose?" Luke replied.

After they finished their coffees and pastries, Luke and Lisa walked up and paid Riaha, thanking her for reaching out to this Brooke person on their behalf. They assured Riaha they would be back at the same time tomorrow, and Riaha said she would do her best to get an answer for them.

Before Luke and Lisa left, Riaha smiled and said, "You two are becoming regular private detectives. Aren't you?"

Luke giggled and said, "Yep, I guess you can say we're a combination of The Hardy Boys and Nancy Drew."

Riaha looked at him, puzzled, and replied, "Who?"

Luke laughed, amused, and replied, "Your youth is somewhat ... disturbing."

Riaha laughed and said, "What are you talking about?"

"Nancy Drew and The Hardy Boys were two different book series of kids solving crimes ... think Scooby Doo in book form instead of cartoons."

"Oh, now I get it! I've just never heard of the other two before," Riaha said, laughing.

Luke looked at Lisa and said, "Never heard of Nancy Drew but knows Scooby Doo. You were deprived as a child, weren't you?"

Lisa laughed, smacked Luke on the arm, and said, "Stop messing with her. Don't you feel sorry for me, Riaha? It's like this all the time!" Lisa said, giggling.

"Yeah, I kinda do!" Riaha chimed in, playing along. "Now get out of here and remember, don't forget tomorrow, and hopefully, I'll have an answer for you."

"We will. We promise," Lisa said as they walked toward the door.

Thirty minutes later, Luke and Lisa pulled up to the house that was the home base for the local newspaper where Tessa works. After walking in and seeing the same secretary at the front door, she didn't even ask and called out, "Tessa, they're back."

A few moments later, Tessa walked around the corner and said, "Hey. Come on back. What brings you two over here? You got some tea to spill?"

"Not sure, really," Lisa said, "we were hoping you would know."

Tessa once again escorted the two into the conference room and said, "Take a seat. What's going on?"

Luke and Lisa went over their conversation with the grumpy old man Henry Cobb, and Lisa said, "We asked him about Sarah Harper and told him about the journals. For a split-second, he looked ... shocked, or hurt maybe, like he knew Sarah. Did they know each other?"

Tessa said, "I guess it's possible. Like I said last time you were here, Sarah Harper's family was well off and would not normally hang around with the lower classes, but I guess there was the possibility of a Romeo and Juliet kind of thing going on—a young rich girl hooking up with the poor kid from the wrong side of the tracks."

"Yeah, I can see that," Luke replied. "Mamma and Daddy say no, which pushes her that much closer to doing it."

"Exactly," Tessa replied, "but as for actual proof, there's none that I know of. She was supposedly seeing someone for a short time before her murder, but as I said, nobody seemed to know who it was. I guess it could have been Cobb, though."

Lisa said, "Well, hopefully, we will get a little closer tomorrow. The young lady from the coffee shop is trying to get us in touch with a relative of Sarah Harper's, and if we're lucky, we can get a little more info."

"Is her name Brooke?" Tessa asked.

"Actually, yes, it is. Why?"

"Don't get your hopes up," Tessa replied, "I've tried to talk to her before, and she wouldn't talk to me once she found out who I was.

Maybe you will have better luck than I did since you're not reporters or columnists."

"I guess it's possible," Luke replied.

"I would like to know what, if anything, she tells you," Tessa said.

"Not a problem," Lisa said. "Can we get a phone number, so we don't have to drive all the way over here to be able to talk to you?"

"Sure," Tessa said as she reached into her pocket and handed them a business card with all her contact information on it, "Call, text, email anytime, day or night."

"We will. Thank you for all your help," Lisa said.

"Glad I could help," Tessa replied as she, Luke, and Lisa stood up, and Tessa walked them to the door.

While they walked to Luke's car, he said, "Who do you think did it?"

After getting into the passenger seat and fastening her seatbelt, Lisa replied, "I really don't know."

"Neither do I. I am more confused now than ever," Luke replied, "the answer has got to be in the journals somewhere."

"Yeah, but we've read quite a bit of it, and there's still no mention of who Christof saw on the beach that night," Lisa said as Luke pulled off from the curb and started heading back to the lighthouse.

"We're just going to have to read the entire thing line by line. With all the other mundane things Christof's written about, there's no way he saw the killer and didn't write it down," Luke said.

"I agree," Lisa replied. "The problem is we haven't found it yet."

"Not yet, but it has to be there," Luke shot back, "I just know it."

"Yeah, and if we find the smoking gun, then what?" Lisa asked.

"We'll cross that bridge when it happens," Luke shot back, "first we gotta find it."

Lisa said, "On a whole other topic, we also need to make flyers and update our website to tell everyone how close we are to actually opening."

"Oh, yes, I haven't forgotten," Luke replied. "It seems that every time we get one thing finished, there's something else to be done."

"Yeah, but we're getting closer each day," Lisa replied excitedly.

Luke and Lisa drove back to the lighthouse and spent the rest of the morning and afternoon unpacking boxes, decorating, and making the lighthouse look stunning. After that, they showered, made a nice dinner in their newly remodeled kitchen, and watched television after deciding to take a night off from reading the journal.

Little did Luke and Lisa know that everything was just starting to get interesting.

12

Luke and Lisa awoke to sunshine beaming through their window the following morning. As always, Luke was the first one out of bed and staggered into the kitchen to make their first cup of coffee of the day.

Lisa came into the kitchen a few minutes later and took the cup of coffee Luke was handing to her without a word. "Well, good morning to you, too," Luke said, grinning.

Ignoring Luke momentarily, Lisa took a sip of coffee, then smiled and said, "Good morning," as she gave him a peck on the lips. Lisa walked over to the huge picture window in the living room that looked out toward the ocean and simply smiled.

"What is it?" Luke asked.

"Oh, I'm just amazed that we get to live here the rest of our lives. That's all," Lisa said as she gazed out toward the ocean. "Wanna go up top?" Lisa asked.

"Sure. Let's go," came the enthusiastic reply from Luke.

Luke and Lisa filled their coffee cups and began their trek up the winding staircase to the top of the lighthouse to the lantern room. A few minutes later, the pair made it into what used to be the lantern room but was now simply an open space with cushioned bench seating around the back half of the room.

"I could stay up here all day long and read books," Lisa said.

The pair watched as a seagull landed on the railing outside of the lantern room and began to cackle loudly at nothing in particular. They watched the seagull for a few minutes as it continued to call, and then suddenly, as quickly as it appeared, it took off.

"I know what you mean," Luke replied as he took a sip of his coffee, "I have an idea. We should get a nice telescope, or a set of binoculars mounted on a tripod or something so guests can come up and look at the stars at night or passing ships during the day."

"That is a great idea," Lisa said with excitement.

Both sat in blissful silence for the next fifteen minutes, drinking their coffee and watching a cargo ship head out to sea. Once the cargo ship was a dot on the horizon and both had finished their coffees, Luke asked, "Ready to go back down?"

"No, but we need to," Lisa replied. "We need to start getting ready to go to Riaha's and see if she was able to contact this Brooke person."

"Yeah, let's go," Luke said reluctantly.

Once they made their way back down to the main house, Lisa hopped into the shower while Luke whipped up a couple of ham and cheese omelets. By the time Luke was done with the omelets, Lisa was out of the shower, and they sat down at the table to eat.

In between bites, Lisa caught Luke simply rubbing the table and smiling in amazement. "What are you thinking about?" Lisa asked.

"Just thinking about all the meals that were eaten at this table. Did I ever tell you that this table is original to the lighthouse?"

"No!" Lisa said excitedly.

"Yep, it is. Think about it ... Christof and Anna sat at this very table over one hundred years ago. Isn't that wild?"

"It sure is. You know what that means then, don't you?" Lisa said.
"What?"

"It means that, in all likelihood, a World War II German spy also sat at this table," Lisa said somberly, "somebody whose family probably never knew what happened to their loved one."

"Very true," Luke said, "Which is why we need to figure this out. I think we are closer than the sheriff ever was to bringing someone to justice."

Once the pair had finished breakfast, while Lisa cleaned up the kitchen, Luke went for his shower, which only took half the time it took Lisa. "That was fast," Lisa said.

"Yeah, it doesn't take me nearly as long as it does for you," Luke said with a giggle.

"Yeah, yeah," Lisa said with a smirk, "by the time you finish getting ready, I'll be done in here, and we can go to Riaha's."

"Sounds like a plan," Luke said as he walked out of the room.

Not long after that, the pair pulled up to Riaha's Coffee Shop and walked inside. There were quite a few more people in the shop than there usually were. It was the first time they had seen Riaha and Josephine working at the same time.

Luke and Lisa stood in the back of the line and glanced around at the other patrons to see if there was anybody else there they recognized, which there was not. In a few minutes, it was their turn to place their order. Luke and Lisa paused a moment for the person in front of them to move out of earshot, then Luke asked, "So, did you talk to her?"

Riaha paused for a moment, then a tiny smile spread across her lips as she asked, "Are you ready to meet her?"

Smiling, Lisa replied, "We sure are. When?"

"How about now? She's here." Riaha replied, "But you should know that she insisted on bringing a friend with her."

"What do you mean she's here?" Luke asked, caught off guard.

Riaha giggled and replied, "She agreed to meet with you if you really think you can solve Sarah's murder."

"We're going to do what we can," Lisa said confidently while Luke scanned the customers, trying to figure out which one Brooke could possibly be.

Riaha said, "You see those two women sitting beside each other in the corner booth?"

Both Luke and Lisa turned and saw two women seated on the

same side of the booth and chatting. One of the women had longer blond hair, and the other had shoulder-length, straight hair. "Yes," Lisa said.

"The one with the longer hair is Brooke. The other is a family friend. She wanted to bring a witness to the conversation. Go on over and introduce yourselves. I'll bring your order in just a moment."

"You ready for this?" Luke asked.

Lisa took a deep breath and said, "Here goes nothing. Let's go."

Luke and Lisa walked over to where the two women were sitting. As they approached the booth, both women stopped chatting with one another and looked at Luke and Lisa.

"Excuse the interruption," Luke said but are you, Brooke?"

"Hey, yes, I'm Brooke," the woman replied with a distinct New Jersey accent. Brooke introduced the person sitting beside her and said, "This is Sheryl. She's here because I learned a long time ago not to talk to others about this sort of thing without a witness."

"Hi!" Sheryl replied, "Yeah, don't mind me. I don't know anything. I've just got roped into this for her," she said as she smacked Brooke on the arm.

Luke replied, "You have a different type of accent. You're not from around here. Are you?"

Sheryl let out a loud laugh and said, "Nope, Buffalo. GO BILLS!"

"You guys suck," Luke joked, "Chiefs all the way!"

"Oh my God! You're a Chiefs fan! If I had known that, I would have kept my ass at home!" Sheryl said, laughing loudly.

Brooke said, "Anyway, what's this I hear about you finding a set of journals that could finally help catch Sarah's killer?"

"Well, that's kind of accurate," Luke replied.

Before anybody could say anything, Sheryl said, "Wait, what's going on? If I took the day off and came here for nothing, I'm kickin' somebody's ass. That's all I'm saying!"

"Settle down there, killer," Brooke replied to Sheryl. "So, what would you say is accurate, then?" Brooke said as she motioned for Luke and Lisa to have a seat across from them.

Lisa slid into the booth first, and then Luke took a seat across from Brooke. Once they were settled, Luke replied, "We found a set of journals hidden in a wall that were written by Christof Wolf. In the journal, he explains what happened, but he did not know who the killer was."

"Wait a minute. You're telling me Christof was there. Is that what I'm hearing?"

"Correct," Luke replied, "Let's say ... he was forced to do something he didn't want to do. Anyway, the night Sarah Harper was murdered, he was on the beach and saw somebody running away from the area. He, apparently, checked on Sarah, but she was already gone."

"And he just left her there? My God!" Sheryl snapped in her thick Buffalo accent.

"Apparently so," Luke replied, "He didn't want to be implicated in her murder. Since he wasn't well-liked by the community, he was scared of being a scapegoat."

"So, why did you want to talk to me?" Brooke asked in her equally thick but distinctly different Jersey accent.

Lisa said, "From what we've heard, Sarah was ... shall we say a partier."

"That's a nice way of saying she had a new flavor every week. From what I've heard, by today's standards, she was downright slutty," Brooke replied.

"Well, we didn't want to say it like that, but yeah," Lisa said.

"From what I've heard about her, for a time, she did like to party, but the last month or so before she was murdered, I happened to know that she found somebody she really liked."

"Who was it?" Luke asked.

Brooke's following words hit Luke and Lisa like a baseball bat in the chest, "I don't know—"

At that moment, Luke and Lisa's excitement completely evaporated before Brooke's eyes. Luke all but blurted out, "How could you not know?"

"What do you want from me? It was over eighty years ago ... but before I was interrupted, I started to say I don't know for certain, but I have an idea who it may have been."

Sheryl's eyes widened, and before Luke or Lisa could say anything, Sheryl snapped, "My God! You do? Sorry, I'm just supposed to be here for support."

Luke and Lisa laughed, and then Luke asked, "So, who do you think it was?"

Before Brooke could answer, the bell on the front door opened, and two older gentlemen walked in. One Luke and Lisa recognized as Harry Crawford since Riaha had introduced him to the couple on one of their previous trips to the shop.

The other gentleman, though, was unfamiliar to Luke and Lisa. "Oh, great. Here comes trouble." Brooke said as she rolled her eyes.

"Do you mean council member Crawford?" Lisa asked.

"No, the one with him. His name is Frankie Mitchell."

"Why do you say that?" Luke asked.

"There's something not right about that whole family dynamic. Most people in town won't say it out loud, but there's some sneaky stuff going on there."

Luke pressed Brooke for more answers, asking, "What do you mean?"

"I don't know, really. It's kind of funny, though, how Frankie started off as a council member and then became the mayor for a time, and then he went back to being a council member. Then, guess who happened to be the next mayor after him... none other than his son. It's a regular old boys club around here."

"Isn't that the same thing that happened with the sheriff?" Lisa asked.

"Yep," Brooke replied, "like I said, regular old boys club around here."

"Now, I see said the blind man," Luke replied.

Sheryl said, "So, Brooke, tell us, who do you think Sarah's new boyfriend may have been."

Brooke said, "Personally, I feel like it was somebody known to the community, but somebody Sarah wouldn't normally have been involved with. Usually—"

"Hello, everyone," Henry Crawford said, interrupting their conversation as he walked up with Frankie Mitchell, "I don't mean to intrude. I just wanted to introduce Frankie here to the Wolfs." Crawford said, "Mr. and Mrs. Wolf, this is Council member Frankie Mitchell."

"Hello," Frankie replied as he shook hands with both Wolfs. Then he looked at Brooke and said, "It's a pleasure as always."

An uneasy silence fell over everyone as Brooke ignored Frankie and took a sip of her coffee. "Well, we will let you all get back to your conversation," Crawford replied. Come on, Frankie, let's go."

Frankie smiled and said, "It was great to see everyone," in an underhanded tone that suggested to Luke and Lisa that there was more to the situation than met the eye.

Only after Crawford and Mitchell walked out of the shop did Luke and Lisa feel the tension start to drop. "Okay, so what was that all about?" Luke asked.

"You noticed, did you?" Brooke replied.

"Yeah, it was kind of hard to miss," Luke replied. "What is it between you two?"

"It kind of goes along with all of this," Brooke replied as she motioned with her hands to encompass the table.

"What do you mean?" Lisa asked.

"We can't prove it, of course, but I grew up hearing stories that there was a good possibility that one of those two that just left either knows or is covering for the killer. Nobody can explain it, but you saw him. He's just ... creepy." Brooke said.

"And that's another reason I came," Sheryl replied, cackling, "I'm her Buffalo backup!"

Luke said, "So, let me get this straight. From all accounts, Sarah Harper was a party girl, but the last month or so, possibly more, she was a one-man woman."

"Correct," Brooke replied.

Lisa replied, "So, that would tend to make me believe that she found a guy she really liked but, for some reason or another, didn't want anybody to know about it."

"Also correct," Brooke replied.

Cheryl asked, "Well, could it have been someone from the wrong side of the tracks? Somebody the family wouldn't have approved of?"

"That is entirely possible, I guess," Luke replied.

Just then, Luke's eyes widened, and he said excitedly, "And I know who it is!"

HARRY CRAWFORD and Frankie Mitchell walked out of the coffee shop without saying another word to each other. Instead, they glanced at one another as if they were thinking the same thing ... *we need to have a private conversation.*

Both men walked to Harry's nearby vehicle, which was a high-end Lincoln Navigator, and hopped in. Before even pulling out of the parking space, Harry pulled out his phone and dialed, turning the speakerphone on so Frankie could also hear.

The phone rang a couple of times, and then both men heard a distinct "Hello" coming through the phone.

"You're on speaker with me and Frankie," Crawford said, "things are getting dicey again. We need to meet."

The phone was silent for a moment, then said, "The usual spot ... two hours."

"Two hours it is. Should we tell Eddie?"

The voice was again silent for a moment and then said, "No, I will handle him." After that, there was a click as the line went dead.

TWO HOURS LATER, Frankie Mitchell pulled up to the hunting cabin, a thirty-minute drive from town. His parents had left the cabin to Frankie in their will after they both passed. It was old and dated, with furniture that appeared to be from the 1960s, but it had all the amenities of everyday life. Heat, AC, cable television, running water, and even internet, although it wasn't the fastest.

Pulling into the driveway lined with rocks, he found that he was the last one to arrive. He parked and walked inside to find Harry Crawford and Tom Baxter already seated at a table.

Both men turned to watch Frankie walk in, and Tom Baxter said, "It's about time you got here. What gives?"

"Sorry, fellas, it took me longer to get away than I thought," he said as he took a seat at the table.

Frankie glanced at Harry and asked, "Have you told him anything yet?"

"Told me what?" Tom asked, "None of us are getting any younger. Tell me already, damn it!"

Ignoring Tom for the moment, Harry replied, "No, I was waiting for you to get here."

Tom waved a hand in front of them and said, "Hello, you two! I'm right here in front of you!"

"Hold your horses, you old bastard," Frankie said. "I was just seeing if you knew anything first."

"I have no idea what in the hell is going on. Can we just get on with it? My grandkid has a baseball game I need to get to."

Both Frankie and Harry laughed at Tom for a moment, and then Frankie said, "Okay, here's the scoop. Earlier today, Harry and I went to grab a cup of coffee at the usual place. Well, when we walked in, we saw the new owners of the lighthouse sitting with a member of the Harper family and deep in discussion."

"So what? That means nothing," Tom replied.

Frankie continued, "And, as you have probably heard, the new owners found a set of journals supposedly written by Christof Wolf."

"It still means nothing," Tom replied, "There is no proof of anything. It's been over eighty years, for God's sake. Even if something incriminating was in the journal ... without proof, it's just words in a book."

"True, but somebody's connecting the dots because they knew to talk to that blonde at the coffee shop today," Harry replied.

"So, what do you want to do?" Tom asked.

"Do you have any contacts on the wrong side of the tracks?" Harry said to Tom.

"Not anymore. All the people I knew are either in jail or dead," Tom replied, "and with my bad hip, I can barely manage to get up the steps at home."

Frankie and Harry burst out laughing at Tom, who flipped both the bird and said, "It's not funny! My wife hounded me for a year to get it replaced before she passed."

Frankie replied, "I may know somebody who can help clean this mess up."

"Good, you don't need me then," Tom said. "I have to get out of here so I can get to the game, and I gotta make a stop at the post office first. You two work it out."

With that, Tom got up and walked out. Moments later, Harry and Frankie heard Tom's car crank up and slowly pull out of the driveway.

Once they knew Tom was gone, Harry said, "I think it's time."

A sneaky grin crossed Frankie's face, and he said, "So do I, my friend ... so do I."

"Is the plan in place?"

"It's been ready for a long time ... just been waiting for the right opportunity to present itself," Frankie replied with a devious grin.

13

After leaving Brooke and Sheryl at Riaha's, Luke and Lisa walked out to their car and hopped in. Lisa asked, "So, who do you think the boyfriend could have been?"

"You're not going to believe me," Luke replied.

"Probably right, but tell me anyway," Lisa smirked.

Luke said, "What if it was Henry Cobb?"

"The crusty old bastard from Riaha's shop? I doubt that," Lisa croaked.

Luke added, "Think about what Brooke just told us. A kid from the wrong side of the tracks that mommy and daddy would not have approved of. Not to mention, this could be the reason the old man is so bitter and angry."

"I guess it's possible. Eighty years ago, the old man was probably very different." Lisa conceded. "I don't know, though. I kind of agree with Tessa. My money is on the doctor. I think with his parents being doctors, he would have the skills to kill somebody quickly, and he would have had the most to lose, and his family name would be ruined."

"Yeah, I see where you're going with it, but I don't know. I just feel like the boyfriend was Henry Cobb," Luke replied.

"You know what that means. Don't you?" Lisa asked.

"Yep, we have more reading to do," Luke said with a smile, "there's gotta be something in those journals we can use to narrow it down a little more."

"I agree with you. Let's go find out," Lisa said with a smile.

Not long after pulling back up to the lighthouse, Luke and Lisa grabbed a couple of the journals that had not been read yet and went up to the lantern room at the top of the lighthouse. There, they settled in, and both started reading.

In a few moments, the only sounds were the occasional pages being turned. For the next hour straight, not a word was spoken between the two as they read, taking in every word Christof wrote as if history was literally coming alive before their very eyes.

"I haven't seen much lately," Luke replied. "There's a lot in this journal, but not much about what was going on. There's just a bunch of stuff about the end of the war, troops coming home, and stuff like that. There's not much about the lighthouse or anything concerning what we're looking for."

Lisa smiled excitedly and replied, "I am having a little better luck. It would seem that there are rumors floating around the town that Christof helped German spies come ashore during the war. From the way this reads, he is being ostracized by a lot of people in the town, even more than usual. There are even talks about a break-in at the lighthouse and the town council members making trouble for Christof."

"Are you serious?" Luke asked, shocked. "Is this before or after the war ends?"

"In the journal I'm reading, Christof talks about the end of the war in sight and how he hopes his surviving family back home in Germany is ok. He writes how he is deeply concerned for his family members living near Berlin and how he hopes they flee west toward the American lines and away from the Russians.

"That means it's at the very tail end of the war," Luke replied.

"Yeah, and that's when the rumors really pick up about Christof helping to bring at least one German spy ashore," Lisa said.

"You may be getting close to something," Luke said, "keep reading and see what you can find."

"Oh, don't you worry. I'm going to stay up here all day and read this entire journal if I have to," Lisa replied with a smile.

"It's curious how things started to go downhill *before* the seven returned home, though. I would have thought it was after they came home." Luke confessed.

"Me too," Lisa replied, "unless ..."

"Unless what?" Luke asked, "Don't keep me hanging," he begged.

Lisa said, "It's going to take some more reading, but it means that the person or people who started the rumors about Christof helping the spy must have already been in town."

Luke countered, "But at this point, nobody else knows about what happened. If what we assume is correct about the killer being one of the Smugglers Cove seven, then the only people there that we know of were Christof, the killer, Sarah Harper, and the spy. We know the spy didn't say anything, and Sarah's not talking, soooo," her voice trailed off as she scratched her head.

"Maybe one has nothing to do with the other?" Luke surmised.

"What do you mean?" Lisa asked.

Luke thought for a moment and replied, "Well, what if somebody managed to put it together that Christof really did help the spy come ashore?"

"Ok, but the war was almost over at this point. Why start making trouble for the guy now?" Lisa asked.

"I have an idea why, but I want to research it more first," Luke replied, "I need to go downstairs and hop on the computer for a while."

"Ok, well, you know where I'll be," Lisa said with a smile. "Oh, by the way, I have a neat idea I just thought of."

"I'm scared to ask," Luke replied, "but what is it?"

"Maybe we could make a pully system or a dumbwaiter for up here. In case a guest wants a drink or something. We could also have a call button installed for the guests to push a button for a drink or something."

Luke laughed and said, "That sounds pretty cool, expensive, but cool. Now get to reading."

ONE SATURDAY MORNING, bright and early, Christof got up and drove into town to pick up some supplies for the lighthouse and some groceries Anna was running low on. As he entered the store, the bell atop the door dinged as usual, and moments later, Christof's friend Joseph came out of the back room.

"Christof! So good to see you! Do you need anything specific or just shopping?"

"It's good to see you as well! I'm just getting some supplies for Anna and the lighthouse. I won't be long."

"Take your time," Joseph replied.

After fifteen minutes of walking up and down the aisles, Christof had accumulated an armful of items, took them to the counter, and returned for a few more things. When he was finished, he waited for Joseph to add everything up, and after a moment, Joseph said, "That'll be $1.50. Want me to put it on your tab?"

"No, thank you. I will just pay for it, Christof replied.

"Are you sure?" Joseph asked, "That's quite the haul this morning."

Christof smiled, pulled the money out of his pocket, and said, "I want to pay for it. No need for the tab."

Joseph took the money reluctantly, then said, "Thank you. This will really help."

"Why's that?" Christof asked.

Joseph shrugged and said, "People aren't paying their tabs as fast as they used to. I'm trying to be patient, but I have bills as well."

"Well, that's another reason why I am going to pay you today," Christof said with a smile.

"Thank you," Joseph said quietly as he helped Christof to the truck with his order. After helping Christof load his order, Joseph said in a serious tone, I want to ask you a question, and I want you to be honest with me, my friend."

Joseph took a deep breath, and as he was about to say something, both men heard another car coming down the street. On instinct, they both looked up to see the sheriff's car slowly approaching the store.

"Well, I guess I had better be off," Christof said as he glanced in the direction of the sheriff's car. Joseph watched as Christof hopped into his truck, backed out, and started down the road.

Sheriff Baxter pulled up in front of the store and, as he hopped out, asked, "Was that the German?"

Shaking his head in agreement, Joseph replied, "Yeah, that was him. He was just picking up some supplies. Do you need something sheriff?"

"No, I was just coming by to chat a little, that's all, Baxter replied as Joseph watched Christof drive off.

"What's the matter?" Baxter asked.

"Nothing, just thinking," Joseph said as he watched Christof's truck turn the corner and disappear out of sight.

"What are you thinking about?" Baxter asked.

Without answering directly, Joseph replied, "Come on, let's go inside and talk."

Both men walked into the shop, and Baxter asked, "What's on your mind?" Was it something about the German?"

Slightly irritated, Joseph replied, "His name is Christof Wolf, not the German. But I wanted to ask if you ever found anything about the Harper girl."

"Nope, I've looked and looked. Nobody seems to know a thing. Several of the girls her age thought she was seeing somebody, but nobody knew who. Why do you ask?"

"No reason. Would anybody benefit monetarily if something happened to her?"

"Now, that is a strange question to ask. Why in the hell would you ask me that?" Baxter asked, his curiosity piqued.

"Oh, I don't know really. There doesn't seem to be any other reason for Sarah's murder. I just wondered if somehow it was related to money."

"I don't see how," Baxter replied, "She was just twenty and still stayed at home. She didn't really have any money of her own. Her parents had money, but this was not a kidnapping or anything if that's what you were hinting at."

Joseph rubbed his chin and said, "Yeah, it was just a thought," as he stared into space.

"What's with you this morning?" Baxter asked.

"Oh, nothing. Still haven't woken up good," Joseph replied with a chuckle.

"Are you sure that the German—ah, Christof didn't say something that spooked you?"

"No, he didn't say anything, and I know it in my bones, he didn't have anything to do with the Harper girl's murder, but—"

"But what?" Baxter interrupted.

"I was just going to say that Christof seems to have a lot of extra money, that's all."

"How much are we talking?" Baxter asked.

"Well, he paid his tab off completely last month, and he just paid for his order this morning right out of his pocket. He said he finally got some back pay coming to him, but it sounds unusual," that's all Joseph said.

"That's easy enough to find out," Baxter replied as he turned and started for the door.

"Where are you going?" Joseph asked.

"To the bank," Baxter shot back over his shoulder, "I'll be back shortly."

IT TOOK ONLY fifteen minutes for Sheriff Baxter to drive to the only bank in Smugglers Cove. He was standing outside as soon as the bank manager opened the door, "Morning, Sheriff," Tony Carter, the frail old bank manager, said, "What can I do for you?"

"Mind if we talk?" Baxter replied, "I need a little bit of information."

"Sure, come inside and take a seat in my office. I have to get the tellers situated, and I will be right back."

"Not a problem," Baxter replied with a smile.

A few minutes after walking out of the office, Carter returned, took a seat at his desk, and said, "Okay, what kind of information do you need?"

Sheriff Baxter said sternly, "This is about an investigation, so you can't repeat what I'm about to ask you."

"Sure ... sure, no problem," the bank manager said, nodding in agreement.

"I need to ask you something. Has anybody in town made a large deposit lately? Does anybody have a lot of money that they probably shouldn't have?"

The old bank manager sat back in his chair for a moment, then replied, "No, nothing of the sort. It's the usual stuff. Can I ask what this is about?"

"Like I said, Tony, it's about an investigation. I can't go into details, sorry. But you're sure nobody has made any large deposits or opened an account with quite a bit of money lately?"

"I'm positive," the manager replied.

Sheriff Baxter stood up and said, "Ok, thank you. If someone does in the next month or so ... give me a call."

"Will do, sheriff," Carter replied as they shook hands. Then Carter walked the sheriff out.

After leaving the bank, Baxter stopped at his office on his way back to Joseph's store. He remembered a bulletin recently put out by the state police about tips on what to look for concerning possible spies.

Baxter shuffled some papers on his desk, finally finding the one he was looking for from the Department of Defense. "Here it is!" Baxter said aloud, although he was the only one there. He quickly began to read, "Be on the lookout for military-age men that seem lost, have clothes that might not fit for the area he's in, have the wrong kind of credentials, hidden credentials, or no credentials. Another clue that you may be dealing with a possible spy is that he will be traveling with a backpack, satchel, or briefcase. He could have a slight accent or carry large amounts of currency with no proof of where it came from, such as a bank receipt. If you as a lawman come across such a person, remember they could be deadly individuals and not to be taken lightly."

Baxter dropped the bulletin back on the desk and said, "Well, that was useless, most of it anyway," as he walked back out to his car and drove off.

A few minutes afterward, the sheriff pulled up to Joseph's store again, got out, and walked inside. "Well?" Joseph asked.

Baxter paused a moment and said, "This is not to go any further because I don't want it getting out that we talked. Got it?"

"Yeah, sure," Joseph replied somberly, fearing the worst.

Even though there was nobody else in the store, Baxter lowered his voice mainly more for effect than anything and said, "It's true. The bank manager confirmed to me that the Ger— I mean Christof, made a deposit for his backpay for taking care of and running the lighthouse."

Joseph smiled and said, "I knew it! I knew he must have gotten that money legally."

"Yeah, well, that doesn't mean that he didn't kill the Harper girl, though," Baxter replied.

THE FOLLOWING SUNDAY, after coming back home from the neighboring community's Lutheran church for service, Christof, Anna, and young Thomas returned to the lighthouse to find a window broken out of the back of the house. Upon entering, Christof and Anna gasped at the sight before them. The house had been ransacked as if someone had been looking for something.

"Who could have done such a thing? Anna asked.

"I don't know," Christof snapped as he cautiously searched the rest of the house, ensuring the intruder was no longer there.

"Should we contact the sheriff?" Anna asked with a tinge of fright in her voice.

Without hesitation, Christof replied, "No, he won't do anything to help us. He probably thinks I'm the one who killed that girl on the beach."

"But you didn't have anything to do with that," Anna replied, almost pleading.

"I know that, and you know that, but the sheriff will never believe it. For all I know, everyone in town, except for one, probably believes I had something to do with that girl's death."

"Perhaps you are right," Anna replied, "what could they have been looking for? We don't have anything of value."

Christof thought for a moment and said, "Yes, we do!" as he left Anna standing in the living room, raced toward the base of the lighthouse, and bounded up the stairs.

Christof blasted into the lantern room and quickly made his way to the windowsill, where he installed a compartment to hide the money that had come ashore with the spy. Christof took a deep breath as he paused a moment before reaching to open the compartment.

Christof noticed that his hand was trembling as he reached out and opened the compartment. Moments later, he was relieved to see that the money was still safe in its hiding spot. Breathing a huge sigh of relief, Christof closed the compartment and walked back down to the ground level, where Anna was anxiously awaiting his return, "Well, is it still there?" She begged.

Christof smiled and said, "Everything is fine."

Young Thomas ran to his room, returning a few minutes later, and said, "My room is just like I left it."

"That is wonderful, Thomas. Now help your mother clean up while I go about fixing the window," Christof replied with a reassuring smile.

For the rest of the afternoon, Christof set out to repair the window as best he could. He didn't have a piece of glass, so for the time being, he cut a piece of wood to fit over the window to keep most of the damp air out.

While he was working on the window, Anna, with Thomas' help for a time, straightened the house up and put everything back in its place. After Thomas' part was finished, he sat at the picture window and simply stared out at the ocean, looking for ships.

Bright and early the next morning, Christof got up, had a quick breakfast, and drove into town to the general store. As soon as he walked in, Joseph came out of the back room and said, "Good morning, my friend. I didn't expect to see you this morning."

Christof smiled and said, "Truthfully, neither did I. Do you happen to have a pane of glass? It would seem we had a visitor yesterday morning while we went to church."

"What?" Joseph gasped.

"I'm afraid so. When we returned from church, we found the window near our back door broken out, and someone broke into our home."

"That's awful!" Joseph said, "Would you like me to contact the sheriff for you?"

Christof shook his head and said, "No, my friend. We know how that will go. Besides, it appears that nothing was actually stolen because we don't have anything worth stealing. Anyway, no real harm was done except for the pane of glass. Let me just get a new pane, and I'll be on my way."

"It's not a problem," Joseph said as he went to grab a spare piece of glass. After he returned, he gently laid the piece of glass down on the counter and asked, "Do you want me to put it on your tab?"

"No, thank you, my friend. This time I will pay for it. How much will it be?"

"That'll be one dollar even for the glass," Joseph replied, "are you still sure you don't want me to put it on your tab?"

"I've got it. I've taken advantage of your generosity too much in the past, my friend. I want to pay you for it," Christof said as he reached into his pocket, pulled out a one-dollar bill, and held it out for Joseph.

"Thank you," Joseph said quietly as he picked up the pane of glass and helped Christof to the truck with it. After loading the piece of glass, Joseph said in a serious tone, "I need to tell you something, my friend."

"Sure," Christof replied as he stared at Joseph trying to discern what Joseph was about to ask.

"This is to stay between us," Joseph said, "I feel bad for something I have inadvertently done to you."

"What is it?" Christof asked, concerned.

"Yesterday, after you left, the sheriff stopped by to chat. We were talking about the Harper girl's murder, and without thinking, I mentioned that you had paid your tab off and bought your weekly supplies with cash instead of putting it on the tab like you usually do. I realized what I had done and made sure to tell him that you got the backpay you had been looking for."

"And what did the sheriff say?" Christof asked.

"He ... said it was easy enough to find out. He told me he was going to the bank to see. He came back about an hour later and said that what you had told me was true. Christof, I feel so terrible for saying anything."

Just then, another customer pulled up. Joseph said, "Go on in. I'll be right with you." The man simply nodded at Joseph.

Christof forced a smile and said, "It's okay. You didn't mean anything by it ... and now you know. You had better tend to your customer, and I need to get going. I have a window to fix."

Without saying another word to Joseph, Christof got into his truck and backed out into the road. As Christof put the old truck in drive, he glanced over to see Joseph throw up a hand to wave good-bye. Instead of waving back, Christof simply drove off as he realized who and why somebody had broken into the lighthouse.

14

"Holy shit!" Lisa snapped, "That means Sheriff Baxter was the one who must have broken into the lighthouse. He had to have put two and two together and figured out the spy came ashore with a bunch of money! I gotta go downstairs to tell Luke!"

Lisa slammed the journal closed and started down the winding staircase to floor level.

It took Lisa nearly two full minutes to make her way down the staircase. She was breathing heavily, but she bolted into the main house towards the kitchen, where Luke liked to set up his laptop so he could look out at the ocean.

"I found something!" Lisa exclaimed.

"So did I!" Luke replied, equally enthused, "You go first!"

Breathing heavily from her trip down the stairs of the lighthouse, Lisa said, "No ... you ... go. It will ... give me a chance to catch my breath."

Giggling at Lisa, Luke said excitely, "Well, I have been doing research on German spies of World War II. In every single known case, spies came with ten, sometimes twenty-five thousand dollars to fund their mission. That doesn't sound like a lot in this day and age, but that would have been almost half a *million* dollars in 1942!"

Lisa said wild-eyed, "That goes along perfectly with what I just found, too! Suppose I just found out who broke into the lighthouse back then."

"In that case, I would be impressed," Luke replied.

"Well, you're really going to be shocked when I tell you who it was," Lisa said.

"Who?" Luke asked.

"None other than Sheriff Baxter," Lisa replied.

"WHAT?" Luke nearly shouted excitedly, "How?"

"Read it for yourself," Lisa said as she plopped down beside Luke.

Lisa opened the journal, turned to the page she had just read, and slid it over to Luke. After silently reading for a moment, Luke gave a long whistle and said, "Damn, that means the sheriff knew or suspected Christof's money probably came from the spy. And since he was now dead, he wouldn't be returning for it, so Christof took it."

Lisa interjected, saying, "And that explains how the sheriff found out. This Joseph fella that ran the store happened to say something to the sheriff, and after he went to the bank, the sheriff assumed the money was at the lighthouse. Not only that, but it explains how the rumors got started about Christof helping the spy come ashore in the first place. The sheriff had to have done it to make Christof look even worse."

Luke replied, "That means we've probably figured out who and why the lighthouse was broken into, but as far as I can tell, that has nothing to do with Sarah Harper's murder, though."

"No, but I'm starting to get what Riaha meant when she wrote on the receipt that not everyone is as they seem." Lisa shot back, "If we keep digging, there's no telling what we might find or who's involved. So, knowing what we do, What's our next move?"

"I still want to talk with Harry Cobb," Luke replied, "the look on his face the other day when we mentioned the journal is enough for me to think that he knows something."

"How will we find him? We don't really know anything about him," Lisa said.

"We don't, but Tessa might," Luke replied as he picked up his cell phone and tapped on her phone number.

As soon as the phone started ringing, Luke put the call on speaker so Lisa could also hear what was being said. On the third ring, they heard Tessa pick up and say, "This is Tessa."

"Hi, Tessa, this is Luke Wolf. I have you on speaker with my wife, Lisa. Do you have a minute?"

"Sure do. What's up?"

"We were wondering if you could tell us how to find Henry Cobb," Luke said.

The phone was silent for a moment, then Tessa said, "Why in the hell would you want to talk to that asshole?"

Luke chuckled and said, "It's a long story, but we believe there's a chance that he may have been the guy Sarah Harper was seeing before she was murdered. If it's true, he may know something."

"I think you're barking up the wrong tree, but if you want to talk to him, he lives in that little apartment complex around the corner from Riaha's coffee shop. His apartment number is 202."

"Got it," Lisa said as she wrote the information down, "thank you."

"Call me back and spill the tea if it's anything good!" Tessa shot back excitedly.

"We will," Luke replied before saying goodbye and hanging up the phone.

As soon as they hung up with Tessa, Luke, and Lisa got in their car and drove into town to see if Henry Cobb would talk to them. They parked in the complex's parking lot and, after searching for a few minutes, found the apartment where Tessa said Cobb lived.

Luke knocked on the door, and as they waited, they both instinctively took a deep breath, unsure of what was going to happen next. After a moment, the door opened, and they were face to face with none other than Henry Cobb.

"Yeah! Whadda ya want?" The old man barked.

Luke forced a smile and said, "Hi. I don't know if you remember, but my wife and I talked with you briefly in the coffee shop."

"Yeah, so?" Cobb snapped.

Lisa said, "Well, we ... we were wondering if you could tell us about Sarah Harper."

On hearing her name, Cobb softened for a moment, then snapped, "She's dead ... been dead for over eighty years! Why do you want to know about her?"

Seeing his reaction to her name, Luke took a shot and said, "You were who she was seeing when she was murdered. Weren't you?"

The statement must have hit the old man like a sledgehammer in the gut because Luke and Lisa saw the old man deflate before their very eyes. Cobb sighed deeply and replied, "Yes."

Softening her tone, Lisa asked, "May we come in and talk with you?"

Cobb simply nodded, backed away from the door, and pointed them toward the couch. Glancing around as they entered, Luke and Lisa felt as if they had stepped back in time. There were old black-and-white photos on a bookcase nearby and an old record player in the corner with a stack of records from the 1940s, among other things.

"So, what's this about?" Cobb asked.

Luke glanced at Lisa and then said, "We are the new owners of the lighthouse, and while we were remodeling it, we found a set of journals Christof Wolf wrote. Apparently, he was turning the journals into a book. Anyway, with everything he wrote, we were able to figure out that you must have been the young man Sarah was dating before she was murdered."

Cobb replied softly, "It's true ... we were in love."

"From what we've heard, she was a little on the wild side," Luke replied softly.

Cobb chuckled and said, "You could say that, but after we met, we were inseparable. We fell head over heels for each other."

"So, why keep it a secret then?" Lisa asked, "Why not shout it from the rooftops?"

The old man smiled and said, "I wanted to, but if her parents found out that she was seeing a working stiff like me, they would have put an end to it immediately, so we had to be careful."

"We kinda figured it might be something like that. So, are you saying Sarah's parents wouldn't have approved of you?" Lisa asked.

"Oh, God no! I was just a mechanic with no future. Sarah's parents had already decided that she was going to marry a lawyer or a doctor... someone who could take care of her."

Luke and Lisa looked at each other with surprise, and Lisa asked, "Did you literally mean a doctor?"

Cobb lowered his head and said, "Her parent's words, not mine."

Both Luke and Lisa sat there for a moment, and finally, Lisa asked the question both were dying to know, "Do you know who killed Sarah?"

Cobb let out a deep sigh and said, "I don't know for certain ... but I have my suspicions."

Lisa asked softly, "Do you mind sharing? We could finally bring her killer to justice."

Cobb sat there for a moment, then stared at both Luke and Lisa and said, "If I tell you, there will be repercussions from those involved."

Lisa looked at Luke, who gave her a slight nod of approval, then Lisa said, "Mr. Cobb ... we're willing to take that chance."

ACROSS TOWN, retired sheriff Tom Baxter returned home from his grandkids game to find the home he had lived in for nearly forty years had been broken into and ransacked.

Before taking two steps into his home, Baxter reached for his phone and dialed his son Eddie, who was actually on duty at the time. The phone rang two times before Baxter heard the familiar voice of his son, say, "Hey dad! What's up?"

In a low tone, Baxter said, "Send a couple of squad cars to my house right now. I just got home, and the place has been tossed."

Had Baxter waited, he would have heard his son say, "Dad, wait!

Even running lights and sirens, you live so far out, it will still be nearly ten minutes before backup gets there!"

Baxter never heard the response from his son before hanging up the phone and sliding it back into his pocket all the while while listening for any sound that could indicate the person was still in the house.

No sooner had he dropped the phone into his pocket than Baxter pulled out his six-shot revolver, which had been issued to him when he was the sheriff. Now that the sheriff's department switched from revolvers to .40 caliber Glocks a number of years ago, his son was able to procure his father's old weapon and surprise him with it as a birthday present one year.

With his eyes up and his trusty service weapon out, Baxter began inching further and further into his home, even though every fiber of his being, as well as his police training, was screaming for him to wait for backup.

After clearing the living room and dining room easily enough, Baxter turned right and started down the hallway when he suddenly heard a noise coming from his office area. Baxter stopped just down the hallway from his office, listened for a second, and definitely heard movement in his office.

Baxter took a deep breath and then darted around the corner into his home office. Seconds later, a shot rang out.

SHERIFF'S DEPUTY Eric Johnson was finally less than a mile away and running lights and sirens to get to Baxter's house as quickly as possible. As he neared the area, he could see smoke rising in the distance and knew it was going to be bad.

As he got closer, it became readily apparent that the smoke was indeed coming from retired sheriff Baxter's home. As soon as he pulled up, Johnson could see thick black smoke billowing out from under the eaves of the house and several windows.

Immediately, he put the call over the airwaves for dispatchers to start rolling the fire department even though he already knew that when the volunteer fire department got there, the house would already be gone.

Johnson jumped out of his squad car and raced up to the front door. He opened the door and was immediately forced back by the heat of the fire brewing inside. He backed away and ran around the exterior of the house, trying in vain to find another way into the retired sheriff's house.

Finally, he found a window in the back corner farthest from the fire. He managed to get inside before being pushed back into the backyard by the thick black smoke that filled his lungs and stung his eyes. Unable to see or breathe, Johnson was forced back out of the same window he had entered only moments before. Johnson heard more sirens pulling up in the front. He staggered around the corner and collapsed in the front yard, gasping for breath.

The next thing he knew, Johnson was in the back of an ambulance with an oxygen mask covering his mouth and nose. Johnson tried to sit up but immediately felt a reassuring hand on his shoulder and heard the paramedic's calm voice saying, "Easy there, you're good. Your O2 was just a little low. Keep that mask on for a few more minutes, and you'll feel better. I still want to take you to the hospital, though."

Johnson forcibly pulled the mask down off his face and said, "What ... what about Mr. Baxter?"

"Well, the fire department has the fire out, but it's not looking good," the paramedic replied as he put the mask back on Johnson's face.

Johnson sat up, took the oxygen mask off again, and slowly started to get up. "Whoa, wait a minute there ... your stats have not returned to normal yet," The paramedic snapped.

Johnson waved him off and said, "I'm good; now back off!"

Ever so slowly, Johnson made his way out of the ambulance and toward a group of people and officers. As he got closer, he could see Sheriff Baxter being consoled by several other people. When Johnson walked up, his face and uniform still covered in soot, he didn't even have to ask... he already knew.

Sheriff Baxter turned in time to see Johnson walk up and, with tears running down his face, asked, "Johnson, how ... how are you? Are you okay?"

"I'm fine. Don't worry about me. Medics said my oxygen was a little low because I took in a little smoke, but no worries. I want you to know I tried. I tried everything I could to get to him, but the heat and smoke were just too much." With tears running down his face, Johnson reiterated, "I just couldn't get to him."

Sheriff Baxter replied, "Son, you almost killed yourself trying to get to him. When your fellow officers arrived on the scene, you were passed out in the front yard and struggling to breathe from lack of oxygen. Nobody can ask for anything more."

"Is ... is he gone?" Johnson asked, even though he already knew.

"There's no sign that he escaped, so it's a good assumption that he's in the house," the sheriff replied. The question is, why?"

"Sir, um ... since he was the former sheriff and your father, should we bring in the state police?" Johnson asked hesitantly.

"No. I'll handle it," Sheriff Baxter replied.

15

Henry Cobb sat back in his chair and said, "After the Japs attacked Pearl Harbor, nobody knew what was going to happen. Germany had already been on a rampage through Europe. After the attack at Pearl, Germany declared war on the United States. Suddenly, with us being on the east coast, everyone was worried about the Germans again."

"I'll bet," Lisa replied.

Without answering Lisa, Cobb continued, "Then a curious thing happened. People in town who normally wouldn't be talking together started talking and exchanging information on what they believed was going to happen. That's how Sarah and I met. We happened to be beside each other in line at a store, and we started talking. Anyway, we were immediately smitten with each other, and it simply snowballed from there."

"You guys met by pure chance," Luke replied, "That's amazing."

For the first time since they had known Cobb, he cracked a smile, obviously thinking about that time in his life.

"Yeah, like I said, though, we had to keep it a secret because her parents would not have approved of me. Anyway, friends of her parents had a kid our age, and since he also came from a well-to-do family, they tried to set Sarah up with him. We were already secretly dating, so she wanted nothing to do with him."

"Sounds like a Romeo and Juliet story," Lisa said, enthralled.

"It truly was, but it was not a story. It was real. Anyway, this ... other person hounded her for weeks. I asked Sarah if she wanted me to handle it, but she said no because she was scared her parents would find out about us. The last time we talked, Sarah told me that she had decided to go on one date with him, and she would tell him that she didn't think they were a good fit. That was the plan anyway. Well, I was not happy about it, but I went along with it."

"Then what?" Luke asked.

Again, Cobb paused, took a long, deep breath, exhaled, and said, "That was the last time I talked to her. After that, she ... disappeared."

Lisa asked the burning question that she and Luke were both dying to know, "Do ... do you know who it was pursuing her so badly?"

Cobb stared off into space for a moment and replied, "I have no proof. It was war, and we were just kids back then, so it was nothing but talk."

"What talk?" Luke begged.

"I wrote it in my letter," Cobb answered.

"Here we go again with the letters," Luke replied, "What's with these letters?"

Cobb changed the subject momentarily and asked, "You know about the Smugglers Cove seven, right?"

Luke replied, "Yes, seven of you signed up together to go fight. Seems like I read back then that if you signed up together, you could petition to be in the same unit."

"That's correct, although it wasn't exactly that way for us. Since I was a mechanic, I was put a little bit in the rear in a vehicle recovery unit. My job was recovering and fixing damaged tanks and trucks— that sort of thing while the others were in more forward positions. As such, even though I was one of the seven, I was kinda the outcast. Anyway, we had no idea what was going to happen, so when we got to Europe and started seeing ambulances everywhere, we all made a pact to write letters home with anything we wanted to get off our chests in case we got killed and never made it home. Well, one of the boys wrote the sheriff and asked him to hold the letters and only give them to the next of kin when we died."

"That seems like the prudent thing to do," Lisa replied.

"Well, for this next part ... keep in mind that nobody knew about Sarah and me seeing each other. We could tell that something was eating one of the boys up inside. He kept having nightmares, waking up in cold sweats ... things like that."

"Who was it?" Lisa begged.

Ignoring Lisa's question, Cobb continued, "Well, after we all wrote the letters, he seemed to calm down for a bit until we got to the front lines. "Well, I only saw the boys every few days after that. Even though we were in the same unit, I was in a different section. Anyway, we were there for a while when it happened."

"What happened?" Luke asked.

"Our unit was sent to Italy, and we had only been there for a month or so when we got ambushed. Anyone who could hold a rifle was manning a gun. It was hell on earth for over three hours as we fought for our lives. When it was over, Dex was dead, and Frankie and Harry were both wounded. They had been trapped in a foxhole with our medic ... Roy Parker."

Luke repeated the name, "Roy Parker ... Roy Parker, why does that name sound so familiar?"

Cobb chuckled and said, "Probably because he's one of the seven."

Lisa looked at Luke wild-eyed and stuttered, "Um ... he ... what?"

"Yeah, he was one of the Smuggler's Cove seven," Cobb replied, "and he is most likely who killed Sarah."

Luke replied, "Holy shit! That means Tessa was right all along. Why do you think he did it?"

Cobb said, "I have no idea who Tessa is, but after the fighting was over and the situation was under control, I helped to evacuate the wounded in one of the heavy vehicles. I saw Harry and he was in pretty rough shape. He had lost quite a bit of blood and was mumbling. I'm not sure if he even remembers or not, but he told me when he was in the foxhole under fire, doc Parker broke down and said he killed her."

"So, you've known the whole time?" Lisa asked.

"Yes, and no. Technically, it's hearsay, but deep down, I knew it already," Cobb replied softly.

"Why didn't you say or do something then?"

"Because it was war, and after the ambush, I was very busy. After the war, we were just so glad to be home and alive. Then Crawford and Mitchell used their local fame to get into politics, and Parker went back to school to become a legit doctor. I guess he's been trying to make up for what happened that night all these years later.

Rumor has it that when we came home as heroes, the sheriff became jealous of our local fame. About that time is when the rumor really kicked off about that German working at the lighthouse, and he helped a spy come ashore."

"I get that part," Luke said, "but what we don't understand is why the sheriff would not give the letters back to you guys when you came home."

Cobb spread his hands wide and said, "Maybe he wanted to try and keep some control of what was going on, and he thought by holding the letters, he could." I really have no idea."

Luke asked, "What about the sheriff's son? Do you think he knows?"

"I guess there's always a chance," Cobb replied, "but my money says he doesn't know."

"Why's that?" Lisa asked.

"Eddie ... that's the current sheriff, was always a good kid. I just find it hard to believe he'd go along with something underhanded like this."

"Unless he didn't know," Luke replied.

"Exactly," Cobb shot back.

"So, if there's any proof at all about Roy Parker being Sarah's killer, it would probably be in those letters," Lisa replied.

"But, if the letters implicate the doctor, why does Crawford want it back so bad?"

Cobb replied, "Because Doc Parker saved his life in that foxhole. That's why. Crawford probably feels like he owes Parker and is going to do his best to make sure nothing happens to the doctor. Now or after he dies."

Luke's eyes widened, and he said, "Because according to the pact, the letter would go to the next of kin after death, meaning it would tarnish everything he's done! That's why Crawford was after the letter. He didn't want his own letter! He wanted Parkers!"

"Tom's not about to hand those letters over to you, especially if there is proof in one of them," Cobb replied.

Luke replied, "No, he won't hand them over to us, but he may hand them over to his son." Luke stood up quickly and said, "We need to get going. Thank you for talking to us."

"You're welcome, just remember ... there will be repercussions because of those letters. Harry and Frankie are still powerful men."

"We'll be careful," Luke replied.

After leaving Cobb's apartment, Luke replied, "You wanna stop in for a cup of coffee? We're so close it would be a shame to be this close and not stop."

"True," Lisa said with a wink and a smile.

Not even five minutes later, the pair walked into Riaha's Coffee Shop. Luke glanced around and saw that there was not a soul in the place except for Josephine, who works occasionally when Riaha needs to do something, "Hello, you two," Mrs. Josephine said in her usual friendly, Sunday School teacher demeanor. What can I get for you today?"

"Just a couple of cups of coffee to go this time, please, both with a splash of milk," Luke replied.

"Okay, now. Where are you guys off to?" Josephine asked.

"We are off to find the sheriff. We need to talk to him about something." Lisa replied.

"You must not have heard?" Josephine replied.

"Heard what?"

"It's all over town already. Earlier today, his father, the former sheriff's house burnt down, and the rumor is that he died," Josephine replied.

"WHAT?" Luke nearly shouted.

"Yes, sir!" Josephine replied, "Needless to say, I don't think Sheriff Baxter will have much time for you today."

"When was this?" Lisa asked.

"A few hours ago. The coroner and fire department are probably still there."

"Smugglers Cove has a coroner?" Lisa asked, shocked.

"Well, in its own way, ya see, when Doctor Parker became too old to practice medicine, he became the impromptu coroner for the town," Josephine replied.

Luke looked at Lisa and said, "You don't say? How convenient?"

"What do you mean?" Josephine asked.

"Oh, nothing," Luke replied as he paid Josephine for the two coffees she placed in front of them. They both thanked Josephine and walked out to their car.

As soon as they got settled, Luke said, "You don't think somebody killed him to get those letters, do you?"

"I don't know, but I am getting spooked, that's for sure," Lisa said.

"Yeah, it is a little … unnerving, that's for sure," Luke replied.

"So, what do you want to do now?" Lisa asked.

Luke thought for a moment and then said, "Let's go home, I guess. We can't take this to the sheriff now. We might have to give it a day or two before we can say anything."

Lisa replied, "You know, if the letters were in that house, it could mean the only proof is now gone."

"Yeah, I know, but we have to see this through," Luke replied as he drove back to the lighthouse.

As the day wore on, news of the previous sheriff's untimely demise raced through the small town, and before the sun went down, there was not a soul in town who didn't know about the fire.

Frankie was sitting in his chair watching television when his cell phone rang. He glanced at the name displayed in large block print and knew this was going to be a rough conversation. Since he was alone in the house, Frankie answered and put the call on speaker, "Yeah, yeah, I know!" Frankie snapped.

"Jesus! Frankie, what in the hell happened?" Crawford nearly yelled.

"My guy was searching the house looking for the letters when Tom came back home and caught him in the act. Tom had his gun already out, but even then, he was too slow. The guy set the fire to cover his tracks and tore off."

"Who was it?" Crawford asked.

"A friend of a friend," came the reply from Frankie, "nobody knows anything."

"And the letters?" Crawford asked.

"He couldn't find them. That was another reason for the fire. Either way ... they're gone."

16

Sheriff Eddie Baxter stayed at the scene of his father's house fire for the rest of the day, simply staring at the remains of his family home. Eddie wasn't even sure when, but at some point, Roy Parker, the part-time coroner, pulled up to the scene.

Parker walked over to where Eddie was standing and simply asked, "Is it true? Was he in there?"

Without taking his eyes off the still-smoldering home, Eddie said, "I'm almost certain he was. He called me just before it happened."

"What did he say?" Parker asked.

"He told me to send a couple of squad cars to his house because somebody had broken in. I told him to wait, but he hung up. By the time one of my guys got here ... the place was on fire."

"Go home, Eddie," the elder Parker replied sadly, "I'll call the boys, and we will take care of him."

Just then, Parker's phone buzzed. As soon as he looked at it, he shook his head and said, "This is Frankie calling ... the boys must know already."

Baxter watched as Parker picked up the phone and said sadly, "Hello ... I'm here already ... yeah, it's true ... I'll take care of it."

"You'll take care of what?" Eddie asked, nearly in tears.

About that time, one of the firefighters was combing through the rubble of what was left of the Baxter home and yelled, "I've found something!"

Several other first responders headed in that direction and started moving debris from the middle part of the house. Finally, one member of the fire department looked around, locked eyes with Parker, and motioned for him to have a look.

Eddie's shoulders dropped as he started openly crying. Before leaving Eddie, Parker said softly, "Listen, the boys are almost here. Are you going to be ok for a few minutes until they get here?"

Trying but unable to form a word, much less a complete sentence, Eddie only managed to nod his head up and down. Parker patted him on the shoulder and said, "I'll be right back."

With tears running down his cheeks, Eddie watched as Parker slowly and cautiously made his way into what was left of Baxter's home. By this time, Eddie heard two sets of footsteps walking up behind him and, at a glance, saw Harry Crawford and Frankie Mitchell walk up with sad looks on their faces.

"Is it really him?" Frankie asked.

Sniffling, Eddie managed to say, "I think so."

Harry said I can't believe it. Out of all of us, I figured he would outlive us all."

A few minutes later, Parker walked back over to where Eddie, and now Harry and Frankie were waiting. As he walked up, Eddie asked, "Well?"

Parker said, "I'm sorry, son."

"Can ... can I see him?" Eddie asked hesitantly.

"You don't want to remember him like that," Parker replied.

Harry and Frankie gently guided Eddie toward their car, and Harry said, "Come on, let us take you home. Nobody will be more respectful to your father than Doc Parker."

Sniffling, Eddie said, "I know, but it's a crime scene."

"Don't worry about that now," Frankie said, "we need to worry about you now," as Frankie once again tried to guide Eddie away from the scene.

Once Eddie was moving toward Frankie's car, Frankie, Harry, and Roy Parker exchanged concerned glances and nods between the three before leaving.

Harry guided Eddie to the back seat of Frankie's car and closed it after he got in, and then Harry hopped in the front passenger seat beside Frankie.

Slowly, Frankie left the scene to take Eddie home. While on the way, Harry's phone rang. He picked it up and calmly said, "Hello?"

Immediately Harry recognized the voice of Roy Parker asking, "Are we on speaker?"

"No," Harry replied.

"Good. Keep it that way," Parker replied, "Does Eddie suspect anything?"

Harry glanced over at Eddie, who was sitting in the back of the car and staring out of the window, "No, he doesn't," Harry replied.

"Good, as far as Eddie needs to know, I'm going to say it was smoke inhalation, but just so you and Frankie know, the actual cause was a bullet to the forehead. Likely, he never felt a thing."

"Thank God for that, at least," Harry replied, "thanks for letting us know." Then Harry hung up the phone.

Eddie interrupted the conversation and said, "Is it about my dad? I need to know what killed him. Please tell me it wasn't the fire," he pleaded.

"Settle down, Eddie," Harry replied. "Doc Parker says it looks like smoke inhalation. The smoke was so thick he just couldn't get out in time. As far as he could tell, there were no outward signs of trauma, which means the smoke got to him before anything else."

"But ... but what about the phone call I got from him saying the place had been tossed?"

"I have no idea. It could be the house was burglarized, and whoever it was set fire to cover up the fact that there was a burglary and your dad just got caught inside."

"Yeah, maybe that's it," Eddie replied, "he should have waited. Why didn't he wait?"

"We may never know that answer," Harry replied.

THE FOLLOWING two days came and went as the town of Smugglers Cove came to grips with what had happened to one of its beloved members. On the day of the funeral, nearly every business in town closed, as most people, including all three of the remaining Smugglers Cove seven, went to retired sheriff Tom Baxter's funeral.

Even though Luke and Lisa didn't exactly know the previous sheriff, they felt they needed to at least make an appearance, which they did.

After the funeral, Luke and Lisa waited for a while to personally give their condolences to Sheriff Baxter and his family. As Luke and Lisa approached the sheriff, Harry Crawford and Frankie Mitchell saw them approaching and moved closer to be able to step in and redirect a conversation if necessary. Luke shook hands with Sheriff Baxter and said, "Sheriff, I don't know if you remember us or not, but I'm Luke Wolf, and this is my wife, Lisa. We wanted to extend our condolences to you and your family."

Sheriff Baxter looked lost momentarily, then said, "Oh, yes. I remember now. You are the new couple that was able to buy the lighthouse. You're turning it into a bread and breakfast place, if I'm not mistaken."

"That's correct," Lisa said, "Well, we just wanted to tell you how sorry we are for your loss."

As Luke and Lisa turned to leave, Sheriff Baxter said, "Just a minute, you two found a set of journals or diaries ... something like that when you were renovating. Didn't you?"

"Yes, we did," Luke replied, "and—"

About that time, Frankie walked up, butted into the conversation, glared at Luke and Lisa, then said, "I'm afraid this is not the time for this conversation."

"Perhaps you're right," Luke replied sheepishly.

Luke and Lisa took this as their cue to leave, and while they were walking to their car, Lisa asked, "What was that about?"

"It would seem that we ruffled some feathers," Luke replied.

"Speak for yourself," Lisa said with a smirk, "I didn't say a thing. So, now what do we do."

"Well, I don't know about you, but I am going to go home and get out of these clothes, then I'm going to go to the lantern room and read for the rest of the day."

"That sounds like an idea," Lisa replied with a smile.

Once they got home, they fixed sandwiches, grabbed drinks, and each grabbed a journal and climbed the stairs to the lantern room.

Luke and Lisa plopped down on the bench-style seats atop the lantern room, caught their breath, and watched as some sort of freighter slowly went by, far out to sea.

While the ship silently moved past, Luke said, "Just think Christof's son Thomas used to come up here and do this very thing."

"I know. It's crazy to think about?" Lisa replied as she opened the journal she was holding.

Luke watched the freighter for another few minutes before he had a chance to open his journal. Lisa said, "I think I may have something."

"What?" Luke asked.

"Hang on, let me finish this part," Lisa said wild-eyed.

Finally, after another few minutes, Luke said, "What is it? The suspense is killing me!"

Lisa said, "You're not going to believe this!"

"What? Tell me, damn it!" Luke pleaded.

Lisa said, "Apparently, there was a whole host of things happening at the lighthouse. Christof writes about two more break-ins and strange occurrences like lights being left on they knew they didn't leave on and sudden inspections from the Coast Guard."

"Sounds kinda like harassment," Luke replied.

"Exactly," Lisa said, "and he writes that everything started a few years ago after the sheriff talked to Joseph at the store back then. He thinks that the sheriff knows about the money and is trying to find it! He knows it's not in a bank, so I guess he figures it's at the lighthouse."

They were both quiet for a moment, and finally, Luke replied, "Are we saying what I think we're saying?"

"Well, if you believe that the late Sheriff Baxter just went to the top of the suspect list in Christof's 'accident,' the answer is yes," Lisa replied.

"That has to be it," Luke replied, "We'll never know now, of course, since the sheriff just died, but what if the sheriff was looking for the money stash and couldn't find it in the house? The only other place to look would be up here." Luke got up and walked over to the sill where the supposed hidden compartment was and said, "The money was in here!"

Lisa said, "And maybe Christof caught the sheriff up here at night before he could find the money. There was a fight, and Christof went over the side, falling to his death."

"There's no way to prove it, though," Luke replied.

"No, but we'll know. Besides, I'll bet if you do a little research, you'll find the supposed trust was started after Christof died," Lisa said. "Anna could have easily told the bank that the money that was left was from an insurance policy."

Luke sat there for a moment and said, "Well, I'll be damned. That does work. I'll have to see if I can check with the bank and see what they say, but ... yeah, I'll go along with that."

Lisa smiled and said, "Well, that's one conspiracy/murder solved! Let's see if we can figure out what happened to Sarah Harper now."

"Easy there, Nancy Drew," Luke said with a giggle, "I've had enough for one day, as he let out a long, drawn-out yawn. "What we need to be doing is getting our website up and running and getting our marketing material ready for the bed and breakfast."

"Yeah, that's true," Lisa replied, "What we really need to do is come up with a name for the bed and breakfast other than the Smugglers Cove Lighthouse."

"Yeah, we'll think of something when we least suspect it. Come on, let's go back downstairs and get to work."

They spent the next couple of days working on getting the house just right, taking pictures of the property, and making a website.

Finally, when everything was prepared, and every T crossed, and I dotted, both sat down and pressed the enter button simultaneously to make their website go live online.

Several days after their website went live, Luke and Lisa had their first booking for the following week. A few days before their first guests were due to arrive, Luke and Lisa worked hard to make sure everything was perfect.

While they were cleaning the glass upstairs in the lantern room, Luke turned in time to see a sheriff's car pulling onto their property and driving up to the lighthouse.

"Uh-oh, this can't be good," Luke said.

"What?" Lisa asked without looking up from the journal.

"A sheriff's car just pulled up," Luke said, "let's go see what's going on."

"I'm not so sure I want to know," Lisa said matter of factly.

Both Luke and Lisa made their way down the winding staircase to the ground floor and walked to the front door. As they approached, they could see a silhouette of two people standing at the door through the frosted glass.

Luke cautiously opened the door to find none other than the current Sheriff, Eddie Baxter, and the current mayor, Toby Mitchell, standing there with serious expressions.

Before either Luke or Lisa could say anything, Sheriff Baxter held up a large manila envelope and said, "We need to talk."

17

Luke and Lisa looked at each other for a moment, then Lisa said, "Of course, come inside. We can talk in our sitting room. Would anyone like a cup of coffee?"

They declined and, as they all sat at the table, said, "You will not believe this."

"What is it that we're not going to believe?" Luke asked.

Sheriff Baxter replied, "First off, neither of you can say anything about this to anybody. Not a word."

Both Luke and Lisa said, "We promise we won't say anything."

Baxter continued, "After ... after my father's funeral, I received this envelope in the mail from him."

Both Luke and Lisa watched with fascination as Baxter opened the envelope and dumped the contents onto the table in front of them. Luke and Lisa's eyes widened as soon as they saw the smaller envelopes which had yellowed with age, and Lisa said, "Are those what I think they are?"

Baxter replied, "That they are ... all postmarked 1942. There's no doubt that these are the remaining letters that the Smugglers Cove seven wrote to my dad for safekeeping in the event they shouldn't come home. As you can see, there are only a few left now."

Luke let out a long whistle and said, "This very well could be the answer to why Sarah Harper was killed."

"And my father," Baxter replied sadly, still shaken by his father's death.

"What do you mean?" Lisa asked.

"If he sent this to me in the mail, it means he knew something was about to happen, and he sent these letters to me for safekeeping. What that means is whatever happened to Sarah Harper is somehow still relevant today."

"I don't know," Luke replied, "her death was over eighty years ago. Why would somebody be concerned about that now?"

About that time, Lisa replied, "Because we found the journals and started asking around, that's why!"

"That is our assumption as well," Mayor Mitchell replied, "also in the envelope was a letter from Tom spelling out his part in this whole conspiracy or coverup or whatever you want to call it."

"Which was what?" Luke asked.

The mayor replied, "Apparently, Tom figured out after everyone came home from the war that one of the seven killed Sarah Harper before they left, and whomever it was probably confessed in the letters."

Baxter jumped in, saying, "That's why Crawford and Toby's dad got into politics to begin with. They wanted to pressure my dad into giving up the letters, but he wouldn't do it."

"As time wore on, everything was at a stalemate ... until we found the journals and started asking questions," Luke replied with a heavy heart.

Sheriff Baxter replied, "And the icing on the cake was when Roy Parker showed up to take care of my dad's remains."

"What do you mean?" Lisa asked.

"Parker has been retired for years and rarely makes appearances. He keeps to himself and stays near home," Baxter replied.

Mitchell replied, "When he showed up and wanted to take an active part in what was going on, it was out of the ordinary for sure. After Eddie here got the envelope in the mail, unbeknownst to Doc

Parker, I called in another coroner from a neighboring town and, well, let's say the cause of Tom's death was not smoke."

Eddie replied, "Yeah, whoever broke into my dad's house shot him and then set the house on fire, either to cover up the shooting and robbery or to burn up these letters."

"Ok, so now what do we do?" Lisa asked.

Sheriff Baxter replied, "Well, now as I see it, these letters are now part of a murder investigation and the motive for my father's murder, so we're going to open the letters. The question is, which one do we start with?"

Luke and Lisa snapped in unison, "Roy Parker!"

"Ok, but first, you want to tell me why?" Baxter asked.

For the next ten minutes, Luke told them the story of going and talking to Henry Cobb and how he thought all along it was Parker."

"That is unreal," Sheriff Baxter replied, "Why didn't he say anything?"

"He didn't have any actual proof, and by the time he did, Parker was a respected member of the community, and his friends were the sheriff and mayor.

"But what I don't get is ... why the coverup in the first place?" Toby asked.

Eddie replied, "Doc Parker saved both Crawford and my dad in an ambush during the war ... they owed him their lives."

All four sat there for a moment in awkward silence until Lisa spoke up, saying, "Before we get to the letters, would anybody like a cup of coffee now?"

"I think that would be great," Sheriff Baxter replied.

"Make that two cups," Toby replied.

Lisa got up and motioned for Luke to come and help in the kitchen. While they were fixing the coffee, Lisa asked, "Should we tell Eddie what we know about his dad being most likely the person who killed Christof?"

Luke thought for a moment and said, "No ... we have no proof, and he's dead now. There's no need to make things worse for Eddie's family at this point."

"That means nobody will know what really happened to Christof," Lisa said. "Are you sure about that?"

Again, Luke thought for a moment and said, "Yeah, I'm sure ... and we'll know. That's good enough for me. Now let's get back in there and open those letters."

Luke and Lisa returned a few minutes later with a pitcher of coffee and a tray of cups, milk, and sugar for everyone.

After fixing their coffees, Sheriff Baxter asked, "Are you ready?"

"Sure are," replied Lisa as she gently picked up the letter written so long ago by a very young Roy Parker.

Lisa carefully unfolded the eighty-year-old letter and said, "It's a good thing I can read cursive writing. Here goes."

Lisa took a deep breath and began to read.

To whomever reads this letter,

Six others and I are about to leave Smugglers Cove, possibly for the last time. We are heading off to war, and if the Great War taught us anything, it's that there are no guarantees. As such, I want to say to my family that I love you all and hope that I can return to you when this is all over, although after what I am about to say, it's probably better if I don't return.

Two days before we left Smugglers Cove, after several weeks of trying, I finally got a date with Sarah Harper. It started off well enough, but when we went to the beach, it turned bad very quickly. I tried to get her to kiss me, but she would not. Finally, she admitted to me that she was madly in love with another person and only took the date with me to tell me to leave her alone. One thing led to another, and I got angry.

I tried to kiss her, and she slapped me. We fought on the beach, and I pulled out my knife, and in a fit of rage, I *killed her. I don't know where he came from, but somebody I do not know chased me off the beach, but I was able to get away from him.*

I sit here now making this vow: I will do everything I possibly can for the rest of my life to make up for what I did that night on the beach.

These are my words,

Roy Parker

Everyone was silent for a moment as they let what they just heard sink in. Finally, Luke asked, "Now what?"

Sheriff Baxter replied, "Well, there's no statute of limitations on murder." Baxter looked at Toby and said, "As far as the other two, it's conspiracy to commit murder at the least."

Toby looked at Sheriff Baxter and said, "This ends with us ... do your duty."

One hour later, Sheriff Baxter and Deputy Eric Johnson pulled up to the home of retired doctor Roy Parker and knocked on the door. As soon as Roy opened the door, he dropped his head and said, "I knew this day would come."

Sheriff Baxter replied, "Roy Parker, you are under arrest for the murder of Sarah Harper. Turn around and place your hands behind your back.

At the same time, in two other locations of Smugglers Cove, Harry Crawford and Frankie Mitchell were also being arrested on charges of conspiracy to commit murder, namely of retired Sheriff Tom Baxter.

After everyone was taken to the small jail, Eddie stood face to face with Harry on the opposite side of the bars and asked, "Why? Why did you kill my father? You all grew up together."

Crawford replied, "We grew up together, but he wasn't one of us. While our boys were fighting and dying by the thousands, your dad got to stay here and sleep in his own bed at night ...that's why. He could not possibly understand the hell we went through, and then he dared to blackmail one of us after what we went through over there. In the end, he got what he deserved."

"And now, so will you," Eddie replied somberly.

EPILOGUE

One week later, the night before their first guest was due to arrive, Luke and Lisa were enjoying a quiet night up in the lantern room and talking about the events of the past week or two when movement on the catwalk outside of the lantern room caught their eye.

Luke and Lisa were astonished to see the ghostly image of a man missing one hand standing at the rail, overlooking the ocean. They quietly watched the apparition for several moments as he stood there simply gazing out at the ocean. Then, the figure turned, looked at Luke and Lisa for a moment, and slowly disappeared before their eyes.

Both stood there momentarily, unable to speak at what they had just witnessed. Lisa finally broke the silence by saying, "Was that what I think it was?"

Luke replied, "If you mean Christof's ghost, I believe you're right. Hopefully, he was coming to say thank you."

"Yeah ... let's say that," Lisa said, slightly unnerved, "hopefully his spirit can rest now that we know what happened to him and to Sarah Harper on the beach that night. The only thing we never figured out was who sealed the journals in the wall and why?"

"My guess would be Anna; we may never know, but I have the perfect name for the lighthouse!" Luke replied.

"Oh, really, do tell," Lisa said as they made their way back downstairs."

"You'll see," Luke replied as he went to their computer and changed the wording on their website while Lisa looked over his shoulder. As soon as he was done, Luke asked, "What do you think?"

Lisa smiled and said, "It's perfect! I love it!"

The following morning, Luke got the newspaper, and, in bold letters across the top, it read,

"SMUGGLERS COVE ONLY MURDER IN OVER EIGHY YEARS SOLVED!"

That afternoon, the doorbell rang, indicating that their very first guests had arrived. Luke and Lisa opened the door at the same time and said, "Hi! Welcome to *Christof's*! And do we have a story for you!"

ABOUT THE AUTHOR

Steven Jacobs was born in 1971 in Wilmington, North Carolina, and at an early age, he became interested in all aspects of history. He became a history buff by watching old movies with his father that contained great actors such as Cary Grant, John Wayne, Henry Fonda, Steve McQueen, and many others.

Later in high school, Steven excelled in United States history, especially in the turbulent years of the early to mid-1900s, and this is where his love for military history flourished. By the time Steven was thirty-five years old, he had read countless books on United States history with a focus on the era of World War II.

At the age of forty-five, he wrote his first book, The Disappearance of U-491, about the disappearance of a German U-boat in World War II. Steven had such a wonderful time writing it that he continued writing and, to date, has just finished his fourteenth book.

Now, at the age of fifty-two, Steven lives in Columbia, South Carolina. He has worked for the government for fifteen years.

Please 'like' and follow his Author's Facebook page for updates and sneak peeks at other books in the works. Also, feel free to leave a review anywhere where books are sold!